*R*AVI
AUT
and oth

A Paperback Original
First published 1990 by
Poolbeg Press Ltd
Knocksedan House,
Swords, Co Dublin, Ireland

This book is published with the assistance of
The Arts Council / An Chomhairle Ealaíon, Ireland

ISBN 1 85371 077 6

"Rest" was originally published by *U* magazine.

Cover painting by Nicki Hayden
Set by Richard Parfrey in Palatino 11/14
Printed by The Guernsey Press Ltd
Vale Guernsey Channel Islands

RAVING AUTUMN
and other stories

POOLBEG

Contents

Margaret

When Donal came home from work that day, the door of the house was open. His wife's clothes lay in a trail all the way to the bathroom and she stood, naked, passing her hand over her belly in front of the mirror. He was about to remonstrate, but she looked up at him and said fiercely, "There's nothing to see. It's got nothing to do with you."

"Are you out of your mind, Margaret? Anyone could just have walked in."

"Well, no-one did."

"You're out of your mind. You should go and see a doctor."

He turned heavily and went out. Margaret heard the clatter of saucepans from the kitchen that was Donal taking charge of his own lunch. She looked at herself again, looked at her well-formed figure, honey-hued. She was the same as ever. It had been a mistake. She turned away and put on her bra and pants and clothed herself in stages from the bathroom to the hall. She stopped at the kitchen door and said, "I have seen a doctor."

Donal was eating baked beans. He looked up. "And?" he said finally.

"He says I'm pregnant," answered Margaret.

Dr McNamara was Margaret's mother-in-law's choice of a doctor, not her own. She did not like him. When she went to him with sickness, weakness, and a failure to menstruate, he smiled knowingly. He went out to perform his test on her phial of urine, and was gone so long that later she suspected him of a little miracle in his dark room. When he came back, his smile had broadened. "Well," he said, "your suspicions are confirmed."

"What suspicions?" Margaret said blankly.

"The test was positive."

"In what sense?"

Dr McNamara seemed exasperated, but Margaret really didn't understand. "You're pregnant," he said finally.

There were times when Dr McNamara was diffident about imparting such information. But Mrs Ryan was a good thirty-five and she had been married three years. And so he waited for the reaction, the joy, the tears. There was a pause. And then Margaret said flatly, "I couldn't be."

"But you are, Mrs Ryan," affirmed Dr McNamara, beaming.

"You must have made a mistake."

Dr McNamara's face fell, then reset stiffly. "Hardly."

"You must have."

"Oh, I suppose there's always a small percentage of doubt. But it's not likely. Are you unhappy about this pregnancy, Mrs Ryan?"

"It's not that…I just can't believe it."

"Most people have difficulty believing it at first."

"You don't understand. I mean I don't think it's

possible."

"But why, Mrs Ryan?"

Dr McNamara was a good friend of the Ryans. She could not tell him that she did not think it was possible because she had not had sex in over two years.

Margaret was thirty-two and stuck in an insurance broker's in Kilkee when Donal proposed to her. It was the only time she'd lost her grip when she said yes. She had struggled against convention, gone for a career, had tried to choose a man rather than let him choose her. But for some months life had gone colourless for her, she had failed to see the point in continuing to struggle. She had just wanted some help, the strength of a man. And Donal had happened along just then, to see her father on business. He had seemed pleasant enough. And the moment of weakness had set her whole life askew. She didn't know why she did anything any more. Life went on relentlessly and Margaret went with it. For Donal, things were easier, because he had always had his life decided for him by his family and convention. He had married Margaret because it was time. But Margaret liked to give her life meaning, and she failed to do this now. The sex had dried up within six months. They didn't have the energy. They didn't like each other very much, anyway. People seemed to accept that life would be like this. Marriage was one of the sodden necessities, complained of but not avoided. And children were the same, but up to now Margaret had at least avoided these.

Donal's bean-laden fork hesitated now before continuing its journey towards his mouth. When he had swallowed, he said, "Is he sure?"

"He seems to be."

Margaret knew what Donal must be thinking and she knew it wasn't true, but she was glad of his discomfiture, glad he would have to see her now as a sexual possibility, availed of by someone else if ignored by himself. She studied his face. But then she noticed something strange. There was a smile forming on it. A smile. "Come here," he said.

She went and stood beside him. He stretched out his arm and then seemed at a loss what to do with it. Suddenly he slapped it round her waist and squeezed her, and released her as quickly again. And then he went on with his lunch. So Margaret realised that far from thinking of her clasped in the arms of an amorous milkman, he fondly imagined that one of the times he was somewhere between falling over her drunk in the bed and pissing himself, he had fathered a child. But Margaret had been wide awake every time, and so she knew better. Wide awake.

And so of course she still believed none of it. There were two more visits to Dr Ryan, who finally suggested referral to a psychiatrist. There was a visit to a women's clinic on Leeson Street, but she still thought they must be doing something to queer the results, and so she bought herself a home-testing kit. To her horror, it too proved positive. That morning she had puked up her breakfast and had sat for a long time with her head against the toilet bowl and tears of effort in her eyes. And so she dragged herself to appointments with Dr McNamara, and sat at home, looking at television, looking at the wall. When she woke up in the morning she fished for the thought that had troubled her sleep—that her memory had somehow failed her and it was Donal's child. But then she looked over and saw his fleshly back turned against her at the far side of the king-size bed. And she knew it was impossible. And her mind ran through the catalogue from toilet-seats to radiation to biological freak to divine intervention.

To divine intervention. The baby moved. Margaret was a spiritual woman, and little by little, as the baby kicked and she grew round, she began to wonder at it all. There had been no physical means by which it could have happened and so, though she scarcely dared to think it...it must be some sort of miracle. Time passed, and this conviction deepened as her body changed of its own will. And she couldn't help but glow at what was happening in her. Her face flushed gold, her blue eyes shone. Even Mrs Ryan senior commented that pregnancy suited her, but Margaret thought, how little you know, Mrs Ryan, it's not the child of your beloved son I'm carrying.

Margaret was a religious woman in a deep, personal sense. She wanted an interpretation of what was happening in her. She liked the local priest whom she had met through the preparation for marriage classes. It was not his fault that the marriage had turned out badly, after all. And so one day she slowly pulled herself and her load up the granite steps and knocked on the green door of the priest's house.

"Congratulations on the arrival-to-be," said Father Mulroney, holding out a chair. "You must be very happy."

"Oh I am, Father," said Margaret, sitting down.

Father Mulroney's hands built a little church on his chest. "Was it about the arrangements for the christening you were calling?"

"Not really, Father," said Margaret. "It's…a more difficult matter."

Father Mulroney frowned. "What would be the trouble, Mrs Ryan?"

"Father," said Margaret, leaning forward and fixing him with her large, blue eyes. "I think my child is…special."

Father Mulroney looked relieved. "Every child is special, Mrs Ryan," he said, and stared into the middle distance. Margaret had to conceal her impatience.

"I know, Father," she said, "but I mean I think my child is a sort of…miracle." Father Mulroney seemed about to observe that every child was a sort of miracle, so Margaret burst out, "I don't know…where it came from."

The words took some time to reach Father Mulroney. Then he frowned again. "I don't understand you, Mrs Ryan."

Margaret blushed, but she beat on, "There hadn't seemed to be anything in the relationship that could have given rise to it."

It was much too near tea-time for this sort of thing. "Surely if there was anything outside the marriage…the confession box…"

"I don't mean that."

Father Mulroney relaxed again. He smiled. "And you say you don't think there was anything that could have given rise to the pregnancy?"

Margaret flashed her blue eyes. "I know there wasn't."

"Well," said Father Mulroney, "sometimes these

things happen without a woman even knowing it. And you're right. It is a sort of miracle, in a way."

He stood up and held out his hand, and Margaret struggled to her feet. The next thing she knew she was helping herself down the granite steps by the railings and Father Mulroney was calling after her, "Give my regards to Donal, won't you?"

And so Margaret could not fail to lose faith in the institutions of the Church. She still went to mass, but she reinterpreted with all possible freedom, because she did not lose faith in herself. In fact, she felt more sure of herself than she had for ages. She bore a great, mysterious hope, and the fussings of Mrs Ryan and the simperings of Donal did not even register with her. And the time grew near and she asked herself excitedly what it would look like. A simple Fogarty, all blue eyes and freckles? Or a gold-haired, gold-cheeked angel incarnate?

And then one morning Donal drove her to hospital because the contractions were coming faster and faster. She was in terrible pain for a while, but it did not last, and her hope just about sustained her. Then she heard crying and they told her it was a boy, but she was craning her neck, trying to see it. After what seemed like ages they put the tiny, wet little thing in her arms and she looked down at it. And as soon as she saw it she knew. It fizzed to her nerve-ends and she couldn't stop smiling. The child was perfect from its tiny closing fingers to its dot-like toes. "It's an angel," Margaret said. The nurses looked at each other and smiled. But she said it again, with conviction, "It's an angel." And they took it away again, and she went to sleep, muttering and muttering to herself, "It's an angel."

***

Margaret's pleasure in her baby was absolute. She never seemed to get bored with the routine of looking after Johnny. Donal poked at him now and then, but Margaret was glad to see he had no real paternal instincts. She took this as proof. But she did not count on Mrs Ryan senior. Imperceptibly at first, she moved in on the new family. She seemed to think it was her right. Soon Margaret's paltry maternity leave was nearly over. There was certainly not enough money to keep her at home. The proposal loomed in the air like a clenched fist, and then suddenly one day, it opened. Margaret was holding Johnny on her knee, looking down into her own blue eyes, looking into a mirror. Whenever she smiled, his face reflected with a wide, toothless grin.

"It's a pity Margaret couldn't stay at home to look after the child herself," said Donal's mother.

Donal sprang in immediately. "Well, it's not possible, that's all. Not with everything we have to pay off. Sure no-one can afford to have their wife at home these days."

"I'm just saying it's a pity, that's all."

Margaret held Johnny tighter.

"What are you going to do with the baby?"

Margaret spoke out. "I suppose we'll have to find some sort of a crèche."

"Not that one at the bottom of the road, I hope."

"We'll have to find somewhere good...with just a few kids..." Margaret's voice grew weak. "Somewhere homely..."

"I suppose these places are to be found, but I hear it's hard to get the kids in. And then, of course, the cost."

"Well, it's bound to be less than what Margaret gets at work. These people have nothing in the way of qualifications," put in Donal.

"Mrs Kelly's daughter pays her place a small fortune."

"Like what?"

Mrs Ryan mentioned a sum and Donal inhaled sharply and shook his head. Margaret grew heated. "They are qualified people. They do courses... I want someone who knows what they're doing to look after my son." Even now she did not appeal to the fiction of Donal's paternity.

"You know what's in the bank, Margaret," he said. Maybe the local place will have to do."

"We could get someone to come to the house."

"Not some sixteen-year-old French girl…"

"Someone who's reared her own family, then." Margaret had grown careless, so much did she want warm arms for the soft body she held.

Mrs Ryan cleared her throat. "Well, I wouldn't mind helping you out for the first year or so."

"Ah, Mam, you've enough trouble of your own without thinking about us."

"You well know it wouldn't be any trouble at all. Sure it would be a pleasure."

"Well," said Donal, smiling, for everything was going according to plan, "I'll have to leave it to Margaret."

Margaret clutched at her baby. She said, "It really would be too much trouble, Mrs Ryan."

"Not at all, it wouldn't. But I'll not force myself on you, Margaret."

Margaret wanted to shout, what do you think

you're doing? This child is the only worthwhile thing I've managed to salvage from my life. He has no relation to you or your family, so keep your hands off him! But instead the voice of her weakest self said, "I suppose you could try it for a few days and see."

And immediately she began to panic. No sooner had she come to love what chance had thrown at her than they wanted to suck it back into the system of meaninglessness. She couldn't bear it. The days went by and the panic mounted. She had the instinct to flee. She began to think, I need a holiday before I go back to work. A holiday...And so one morning it bubbled out of her at breakfast—"I thought of taking Johnny away for a little holiday before I go back to work."

"What?" said Donal, "back to Kilkee?"

"Well," said Margaret, "maybe a bit further west as well, get a bit of fresh air."

"Where would you stay?"

An inspiration came to Margaret. "There's always my aunt's beach house in Mayo."

"As long as the child doesn't get his death of cold." Donal went back to his breakfast and Margaret was jubilant. That night she began to pack warm clothes for herself and the baby into a huge, brown case. And the next morning she was on the train. She did call home for a night to get the key of the beach house, and then she set out again.

***

It was dark. Margaret struggled round the back to turn the electricity on at the mains, and then went inside. Of course it was all much smaller than she remembered. Dingier. It was terribly cold and she held Johnny close to her as she tried to get the wheezing Super-Ser to light. But then it did. Johnny was burbling, then whinging, wanting his feed. She settled him on her knee then, smiling at the frantic way he fed. He lay against her and his eyes began to close. Margaret realised all at once that she was at peace. She lay Johnny down in his carry-cot. She unpacked the picnic basket of food she had brought and soon she was curled up on the couch with a cup of tea. A gust of wind blew the mandatory rain against the pane, the Super-Ser hiccoughed, but Margaret felt secure. The bedrooms were gelid and so Margaret camped in the kitchen, drying out blankets far into the night. She slept long and deeply, and the baby breathed gently beside her.

The peace and warmth grew and deepened, that was what happened. Margaret cleaned and aired the little house bit by bit. The days slipped by without her even realising, and soon she refused to realise. On the sixth day the postman hurtled down the track and handed her a letter over the stone wall. It was from Donal, asking her to phone him to say when he should meet her from the train. She was due to go back to work on the Monday and so on the Saturday afternoon she hitched into the nearest town to telephone. She carried Johnny in a pouch in front of her, she walked through the streets, and the wind gushed up the side-alleys from the sea. She felt well. She saw the post-office sign and went towards it, but then she thought, look around the town before ringing Donal. And it was really when she saw the tarred paper that it all began in her. She fingered it; the man was helpful. He asked her what she wanted it for and she said she was just looking. It was great protection, he said. That was what she wanted it for exactly. Protection. What kind of a house did she have at all? A beach house? Ah, she'd need it alright, but it wouldn't look very nice, mind. Would it make the house warmer? she asked. Warmer? said he. As warm as toast. Oh, and then she began to think back on the little kitchen and the couch bed, and the baby sleeping peacefully. And then she was buying the tar-paper, huge amounts of it, a hammer, nails—arranging for them to be delivered. She went to the post-office to ring Donal and tell him she would be staying another week, then she walked past it, she stuck out her thumb. As luck would have it a car pulled up, and she found herself speeding back to her little house, discussing the weather.

On the Wednesday of the next week the tar-paper arrived, and it was on the Thursday, as the baby slept inside, and she swayed on a ladder hammering sheets of it to the bare wood of her walls, that she heard the car slow. She climbed quickly down and went inside to look through the front window. Yes, it was Donal. And so the time had come and she would have to go back to him. Johnny sensed the tension and began to cry. Margaret saw her husband appraise the house with distaste, and then the gate opened again, and Mrs Ryan senior entered and navigated the rough path, leaning on her son's arm. Margaret took Johnny into her arms, and miraculously, he stopped crying. She held him tight, and it was the moment she met Mrs Ryan's eyes that she decided. She was not going back.

The meeting was acrimonious, Mrs Ryan putting

in her fair share, of course. Whenever Donal said "our son," Margaret felt like laughing in his face. But he didn't lay a finger on her, and she was thankful for that. He ranted on about the good job she was losing, about court cases, but Margaret stood her ground and pretty soon she realised that Donal was frightened. She offered them a meal and beds for the night, but they declined. Instead, they turned and got into the car, and drove straight to Dublin in the late evening—pure madness, as anyone could have told them. Margaret shut her door and began to smile. She had never thought of leaving Donal before the baby came, because she had been too depressed to imagine that things could get better. Now she was in charge again and it felt good. The next day she was up a ladder, hammering in the tar-paper, so that the house looked like a black igloo, featureless on the outside, but dry and warm within.

There were visitations and communications, but then Margaret realised it was all about money, and was astonished. She told Donal she wanted nothing, just freedom and solitude. She knew he wouldn't mind not being able to marry again. In the eyes of the world he had done his duty as a man, he had married and fathered a child; only Margaret knew the baby was not his. And she began to think, for she had grown philosophical, that no-one should claim a physical link with a child to whom they did not have a moral commitment. Mrs Ryan soon moved into Donal's house, and cooked him up his breakfast as she had always done before Margaret. There were to be two more visits every year, which seemed fair enough, and everyone grew contented.

Margaret did a mixture of part-time work. She sold home-baking, she did some cleaning, she looked after other people's children, which provided company for Johnny as he came to need it. She made very little money of course, but they managed, and she certainly did not miss her job typing up affidavits for Donal's best friend. She got on quite well with the neighbouring women. One of them showed by a sparkle in her eyes here and there that she approved of what Margaret had done. Once after a whiskey or two she even said, "Margaret, I often think of you as the new sort of mother...the way mothers will be in the future. Or maybe the way they were in the past..." As for romance, the local men took an interest in her, lovely woman that she was, and one night there was a knock on her door. But she didn't answer. She had long since shut down her hopes of getting pleasure from a man, and like a deprived plant, she concentrated all her power on keeping her one root in its layer of dust.

Johnny was all Margaret's joy. He was a beautiful child with rowdy blonde hair and an impish grin. Margaret thought he was beautiful, anyway. She was an intelligent woman and right from the start she tried to teach him whatever she knew. He was three years old now and he would question her from one end of the strand to the other and back again. Margaret did not get irritated because she was not tired or anxious. And sometimes Johnny asked questions which she could not answer and so together they set about finding out. It was very rarely the Margaret missed the presence of a man. She knew this situation was not ideal, but it seemed the best she could offer. Certainly up to now Johnny had seemed to find even the twice yearly visits to the Ryan stronghold in Dublin too much. He did not respond to Donal's few playful punches, and Margaret felt that even if they had lived together, it would have been no different, for the child had a sure sense of who really cared about him. For Margaret, the visits were merely embarrassing. There was usually one speech from Mrs Ryan designed to re-awaken Margaret's sense of her wifely duties. But it grew less and less committed as time went by, because everyone was really much happier with things as they stood. Donal and Mrs Ryan bought Johnny sweets and toys, it was the only way they knew of expiating their sense of responsibility. Margaret ached, but she put up with it, and it was soon over. And up to now it had just left Johnny feeling sick and bewildered.

***

But time passed. Johnny was going on four when they went up to Dublin for the last time, and he seemed suddenly to have got old enough to enjoy it. What had frightened him before, excited him now. On the fifth day Margaret was sitting in the kitchen when Johnny came bolting in and grabbed her by the hand. "Come on, Mam!"

"Be careful, Johnny!"

"Come and see!"

"What, love?"

He pulled her into the garage. Standing in the middle of the floor was a brand new tricycle. Donal was busy re-adjusting the height and Mrs Ryan was looking on in glee. Johnny jumped on it again and went pedalling round frantically, shrieking with delight, "Look Mam, like a postman!"

Oh thank God they were leaving the next day, thought Margaret. She would have to carry the tricycle on the train and what use would it be on the lumpy roads at home? She didn't like the look of Johnny that night at tea, so feverish and excited. Then he wanted to stay up and watch television afterwards and cried when Margaret said no. Well, well, it was the over-excitement. He was so tired his eyes were closing as she held open his pyjamas. He climbed into bed and seemed to quieten. Margaret savoured the moment, the evening glow in the sky, the birds calling to one another. "We're going home tomorrow, Johnny," she said softly, half thinking he would be asleep. And there was silence for a moment, so that she thought he was.

But then he said, "I like it here, Mam."

Margaret calmed herself. "But Johnny," she said, "think of Jessie's puppies, and the little house on the beach!"

"There's no toys at home."

"We can bring your toys home with us."

He considered for a moment and then said, "Everything gets lost or broken at home. I lose it on the beach or Jessie goes off with it."

Margaret's eyes began to sting. "You'll feel different when you're at home, love. You can go exploring with Michael Keogh."

"I want to stay here."

"We'll talk about it in the morning."

Johnny dug his little fists into the bed. "I want to stay here!"

"Do you want Mam to go home on her own and leave you with Dad, then?"

She turned and looked at him, and he saw she was crying. And he put his arms round her neck, for he was a gentle child, and said, "No! I want you to live here with Dad... Like the Keoghs."

And this was what happened, in the end. Never would Margaret have guessed that those slender brown arms would pull her back into the system of meaninglessness. But Johnny was only the agent of prevailing forces, which proved too strong in the end for Margaret herself. She understood then that it didn't matter who his real father was or was not, Johnny wanted merely to be the same as everyone else. And she began to equate what he wanted with what was best for him. It broke her heart. But no-one saw or no-one cared to see. Soon she was a quiet, slightly lazy woman, going on forty. Although the years in the west were referred to, rather ridiculously, as "the holiday," they had been Margaret's only real taste of living. She still loved her little son of course, but he pained her too. He reminded him of broken possibilities. And perhaps later he began to feel he was paining her. And one terrible winter Margaret began to feel sick and couldn't sleep for dreams of something growing in her, unbidden, unexplained. She knew she would have to go to Dr McNamara again, but she couldn't face it, for this time she knew the certainty of celibacy was no guarantee. She prayed to her god for deliverance, even thought of making the forlorn trip to England. This strange miracle was perhaps the only unique power Margaret Ryan had, but she had other, more common powers as well, courage, imagination, passion, and like the unique one they came to cause her only pain, to be a burden she could hardly shoulder, would rather have done without.

Mary's Garden

am growing old and it is time I explained myself. Here no-one understands me. The villagers call me names, sometimes "madman," sometimes "poet," because I can read and because of the quiet life I lead among them. My wife never understood me, but we get along together somehow, we comfort each other. I have never told anyone the most important episode in my life because I'm afraid I'll be misunderstood and found some morning lifeless in a ditch. Things that are false would go on being said and things that are worthless would go on being done.

I don't know why I became fascinated by Mary Magdalene. I told myself it was because of the radiance of her conversion, but I think really it was the magic of her femininity that excited me. I was travelling all over Israel searching for traces of Christ's life, but it was Magdalene I wanted most to see. She proved the most difficult to find. She had covered her tracks almost completely. But a giggling old man, perhaps nursing some disappointment, pointed me towards her village with malicious pleasure. It crouched on the stretch of good land between the source of a small river and its disappearance into rock, and her tiny house was on the outskirts, set apart in a patch of surprising fertility. I knocked on her door and a woman opened. I knew immediately it was she. Seeing she did not recognise me, she made to shut the door in my face, but then she hesitated and stopped. The door opened again. "Come in," she said, "and clean yourself up—then leave."

I followed her inside. She said nothing else, she kneaded bread silently on a stone, and so I found a pitcher of water and washed my face, and drank. Then she said, "Sit down and rest yourself for a moment if you like." I sat on a low bench against the wall and my incredulity at being actually in her presence melted against the sheer fact of my tiredness. My eyes closed, my head sank against the wall. I listened to her hands working the dough and fell asleep as easily as a child.

I must have slept for some hours. When I woke I was lying on a mat on the floor and she was looking at me. I felt so foolish. Here I was on my great pilgrimage and it turns out I push my way into a woman's house and fall asleep on her floor. I sat up and began to apologise, to offer to leave. But then she smiled for the first time. "You can't start without eating. You probably have no money." This was the case. I murmured my thanks and moved to the table. I hadn't eaten for a night and a day. She put bread and soup before me and I ate ravenously, while she went on with her baking. When I had finished everything she had given me, she laughed out loud, she said, "God help you, you're too young to rely on the Lord's provisions. You should find yourself a piece of land and a woman to cook for you before you die of starvation." She looked bitter suddenly. She sat down and poured herself some wine, poured me some more. She pushed a bowl of figs towards me and took one herself and peeled it. "They're too ripe," she said. "I haven't got the energy to climb and pick them, I let them fall—the ones the youngsters don't steal. I wish I cared, but I don't." She looked out through the open door at her small patch of ground. She must have had six fig trees and their branches were dark against the evening sky. The sun sets suddenly in the Middle East, the sky goes purple and orange and the sun drops out of sight. She said, "You can't leave tonight." I began to demur, to offer to go, but she didn't even listen to me—and of course, I was talking nonsense; it was stay with her or under a bush somewhere where I wouldn't have stood much chance of making it through till morning. Wearily she motioned upwards and said, "I always sleep out on the roof in this weather." She was setting my mind at rest. She had had long experience of men like me. And she knew her reputation. She had become well-known by renouncing her former life, but what attracted people to her story was what they would have called her sinfulness.

I think she knew that. I remarked immediately the knowingness in her steady hazel eyes. Her black hair was piled up on top of her head, her face was lined. But then she came back to the table and poured herself more wine and pulled the knot out of her hair. The light was dim, a single lamp burned softly in a corner, and suddenly she looked young. I found myself wondering was this how she looked when he saw her and loved her. I found myself staring, fascinated by the thought. How was it that she had always lived alone? Her beauty was famous as far as Rome. She met my eyes suddenly. "What's your name?" she asked.

"They call me Peter now."

"One of his followers. You had the look of him just then, grave and simple."

I blushed so much it hurt, I remember, but she didn't notice. She grew serious. "Be gentle with yourself. Don't ask more of yourself than is...useful."

I didn't understand her. "How can I ask too much of myself?"

"Easily. You're fragile, a moment of breath and blood."

"My body, yes…"

"It's all you can be sure of."

"He told us often, the soul is immortal—we can be sure of that."

Well, he said a lot of things. Some of them wonderful. Some of them maybe he shouldn't have said at all."

I was confused, I wanted to run, but I knew it would be wrong. No, I told myself, listen, reason, as Christ would have done.

"Mary," I said. "He saved you. Think of the misery you would live in if he hadn't. That salvation is invalid if you can't believe in his truth."

"I'm no less miserable for having known him. As to his truth, I saw him, I touched him. That was his truth for me."

"His truth is something more powerful. It's what I and a thousand others can feel, though we never saw him."

"That's the power he wanted. He chose death to

attain it."

She was frightening me now. "You don't criticise that surely?"

"Yes, I think I do,"

"You've slipped, Mary," I said. "You've gone back to your old ways."

She laughed at me. "My old ways! What do you know about that? I reject the forgiveness that leaves me open to the superciliousness of twenty-year-olds."

She went quiet. Then she glanced up at me. I probably looked close to tears. "I'm sorry," she said gently. "It's not your fault you think the way you do, nor mine that I think the way I do. In fact, our feelings are probably closer than you think. I've never known a greater man."

She smiled and lay back against the wall. "I remember the first time I saw him, in a market place in Jerusalem. It was as if his body glowed. I wanted to be close to him the moment I saw him, but that was impossible, the crowds were pushing in. I knew where to find him, however. In a moment of intimate relaxation one of the more eminent Pharisees had let slip that the Prophet was dining with him in a few days' time. And so on the day Jesus was sitting in the Pharisee's house, I came in through the side entrance I knew so well, and walked up to him. I had wanted to speak to him, but when I bowed I saw his feet, all cut and blistered from walking endless miles on hard roads. No-one had thought to wash them and so I did, and I rubbed in the ointment I had brought. And because I could find nothing to dry them with, I dried them with my hair."

Her voice was beautiful and I was rapt. I looked at her hair. She had dried his feet with it. Then I reached out and gripped the ends for a moment. She smiled and went on.

"Everything was very simple before I touched him. I was intelligent, I was beautiful, I could afford to dress well. I was laughing at everything and everyone. But he drew me up to my full height and I looked into the eyes of the Pharisees, the people I had played at living with. And I realised I would never play at living again and that they would never do anything else. I followed him then, along with the twelve and many other men and women. I loved him. I deluded myself for a while that he would choose me. But he would never have given one person all his passion, even for a night. He chose death. And of course, having known him, I could never be satisfied with another man."

"He had to fulfil the scriptures, Mary."

"He chose death," she insisted. "He chose his betrayer. I've had twenty years to think about him and I'll tell you what I've come to believe. That the combination of his obscure birth, his poverty, then his genius and poverty, had made him like a vessel, wonderfully wrought, but still a vessel. He could hold the full force of human emotion, and through him there was nothing ordinary people couldn't do. But without their belief he was nothing and could do nothing. Except what he did in the end. He was more in need of love than anyone I've ever met, and for a time my trade was meeting lonely people. He needed love so much he wanted everyone to love him. And when they didn't, he punished them with a sacrifice they never asked for. They could love him now or be damned. Altruism and selfishness are different manifestations of the same thing, you know. I remember that generous man screaming at a fig tree, "Wither!" because he was hungry and there was no fruit on it. And because of our belief in him the fig tree withered. And in the end, because we couldn't enjoy him enough, he let himself be killed off like a sickened tree."

"He wasn't just a man, Mary, he was the son of God. The interpretations that apply to a man don't apply to him."

"Oh nonsense! I was there. He was a man alright. I was there and I saw it."

She leaned close. "Do you know what crucifixion's like?"

I had heard. I said nothing.

After a moment she continued, "It stays with me every minute. And the followers talk about his suffering as if it was something holy! What about the nails going through me still every day? How is it people can shut their eyes to that?' "

The only thing that witnessed to anguish in her was the clenching of her fingers on the edge of the table. I was trembling at the horror of the picture she had drawn. I thought I knew how to quiet her...and myself. "The tomb didn't hold him long. Only three days. That's what we celebrate, not his death."

I was reading through the scriptures in my mind. And then I started, "It was you who found the empty tomb...the grave clothes..." Her look disquieted me, but I went on. "How do you explain that if he wasn't God?" I looked at her again. The expression on her face shocked me, but in retrospect it was one of the most beautiful I have ever seen. It had gentleness in it, with pity and sadness and calm. From that moment I believed everything she said to me, there was no help for it. But old words pushed out of me, "How could you? How could you roll the stone?"

"There was another woman with me, an old friend."

"No! I won't listen. How could you bury him? Where?"

"Near me, not alone in the cold and damp. I didn't want to say any of this, but I can't lie to you. I don't want you to choose death too. Now it's late, let's go to sleep."

"Near you?" I remembered the patch of flowers and vegetables, edged with fig-trees. "In your garden?" I got up and ran out. I knelt down on the earth and sank my hands into it.

She ran after me. "Peter, come inside! It makes no difference..."

"You've been lying to me. I've been sitting here believing you... I'll prove you've been lying to me!" The earth was loose, soft river clay. I plunged my hands deeper. She rushed at me, screaming something, I couldn't tell what. We struggled. I was much stronger than her and it was when I realised this, and how wrong it was to wrestle with a middle-aged woman, that I slowed and began to distinguish her words.

"No, please don't, don't Peter! Don't desecrate my garden, please don't!" I went still and she put her arms round me and said, "I didn't want them to laugh at him, you can understand that. That's why I went along with the story."

"Was none of it true?"

"I saw him afterwards. I didn't recognise him but when he said 'Mary,' I knew it was him. No-one else said my name exactly that way. He said he was going to leave me, but that the place he was going to was my place as well. I believe that. So you see, most of it was true. All that was best was true."

I left at first light. I thought she was still sleeping but when I had walked out over the garden I turned. She was sitting looking at me, smiling. I turned again and went on. I never saw her again. But I forgot nothing. It took weeks but eventually I got back to my village, my family. They had been distracted with worry, but I told them I wasn't leaving again. I married, I had children, I grew reasonably contented. I settled.

Mr Brennan's Heaven

This place reminds me of my convent school. Perhaps it's the cool white walls or the veiled women—but mostly I think it's the face of the Virgin looking placidly down from every nook and cranny. The rituals of life are very simple here, with a gong at mealtimes and at six o'clock the great clash of the Angelus. I feel secure. I can go nowhere, I can have nothing. People are always telling me to get well, that I've everything to live for, that I'm young, beautiful. I tell them I've seen it and I don't want it. I don't see the point in going back to it all.

I'm a married woman and I'm only twenty-two years old. Tony was older than me, he was thirty. You'd think he was dead from the way I'm speaking about him but it's just that I no longer see him. It began that I had no wish to see him, that was a part of my illness. But now I think it's really he who keeps the distance. Perhaps he is seeing someone else. Perhaps he can get an annulment on the grounds of insanity.

It's not that Tony was a bad husband to me, it's just that he wanted more of me than I could give. Everything began to fall apart on our honeymoon. I was very unsure as to what was expected of me. I was certainly too confused to feel passion. I had never been out of Ireland before and I found the heat unbearable, it hadn't come across at all in the brochures. The first day I was stupid, I went out in the sun for the whole morning, and of course my fair skin burned and for a time I couldn't go outside at all. But my skin slowly came to itself and began again, after the botched attempt. Slowly I turned a deep, golden brown. I marvelled at myself in the mirror, my bronze face contrasted so with my fair hair.

I was unsure of the money, frightened of the people and their hard language, and so I stayed by the pool and sunbathed. My tan became an obsession with me, it seemed to be the only thing I could be sure of doing well. I became aware of myself as a sexy woman, the eyes clamped on me as I walked along the pool's edge. At first Tony was pleased to see me looking so well, but soon he realised that I was moving away from him. I had never heard a magazine or a mirror image speak, and so I was unsure how to communicate with him.

It is a shocking thing for a young girl to discover that she no longer has any idols but herself. As a schoolgirl and secretarial student I had found Tony fascinating, with his strong, tall figure, his blue eyes, his big job in advertising. I had been flattered by the older man's attentions, at a loss to explain them. I was clever, the nuns wanted me to join the convent, be a teacher. But I was not considered pretty, I was pale, puny. I was not one of the beauties of the class, the girls one expected automatically to marry rich men at an early age. And my new beauty confused me, I didn't know what to do with it. I didn't know how to relate to Tony now that he could no longer give me anything I couldn't have by myself.

I lay underneath him though, waiting for it to end. Then there was that trip to the Sahara, and Tony insisted I go, as it was three days long and three days is a long time to be away from your wife on your honeymoon. I fussed a lot packing I remember, Tony was impatient with me. You see we'd discussed it all before we ever got married. There were to be no children for at least three years. Then the managing director would go on early retirement and there would be a general reshuffle. Every morning I religiously pressed my white pill from its pink foil packet and swallowed it down. But I brought the wrong bag to the Sahara. There was nothing I could do. Frantic, I brought my crumpled prescription to the one chemist in the village, but they just looked at me disdainfully and shook their heads. Three days passed. I couldn't tell Tony, he hated that sort of thing—disorganisation, mismanagement. Then later I was meant to bleed and I didn't, though of course, as I told myself, there were so many other possible reasons, the climate, the food, the anxiety itself. I couldn't cope with or understand the idea of a baby, and this closed the chink that had remained open between myself and my husband. I could tolerate his love-making no longer.

Sometimes I worried about what was happening to my personality. Then I would say to myself, this is an aberration, this will not last. In Ireland, things will be different. I thought then of the shining new house, its new pots and pans. I thought that once back in Ireland I could learn to make a home for Tony. I pined then for the cool, dull days, the friendliness, the banality. I could be more like myself sipping whiskey on the high stool of an old pub on a quiet afternoon. I think Tony felt all of this too and he held my hand as we approached Dublin airport at dawn one morning. The familiar sights rested me on my way home in the taxi, and I felt a great sleepiness come over me. We went to bed and I remember holding Tony as I fell asleep. Then after four we closed the door of our sparkling new house and walked arm in arm into the city centre towards the pubs.

We chose Brennan's at last, one of Tony's favourites from his student days. We pushed the door open and found the dark pub still silent after holy hour, the ashtrays shining, the water-jugs brimming, the barman standing waiting in the shadows. We sat on high stools facing the big brown arch which stretched up to the ceiling in a series of voluptuous curves and spirals. Tony ordered two whiskeys and we sat back and savoured the silence. I looked into the mirror facing me, which gave back the upside-down spirit bottles and then the whole pub, embossed with the golden letters of a whiskey advertisement. Some more people entered and suddenly I noticed that the barman was staring at me in the mirror as he tapped in the measures. I stared back but it was no good, his eyes strayed to me again every time he turned to the tap. There was a fierceness in his eyes, as if he was counting something in my face, giving up, starting again. I began to look closely at myself and then I understood what had happened. The holiday had put heaven in my face, a heaven far beyond the calculations of a simple barman. Tony ordered another round and the barman wrested himself away from the mirror to place the drinks before us on the marble. Tony paid and the coins rattled into the till.

The barman leant against the shelves and folded his arms across his middle. He looked at me briefly again and then turned to Tony: "Ya didn't get that tan in the back garden."

Tony leaned over and took my hand and then opened his fingers to display my gold ring. "We've just been on our honeymoon in Tenerife." The barman muttered something about how lucky Tony was. Tony nodded and raised his glass. "It's great to be back all the same."

The barman chuckled ironically. "It is?"

"Well, you know," said Tony. "We've a lot of work to do on the house. It's going to be nice to settle down to normal life together."

"You're settling here, so. You'd never try England."

"I was over there for a couple of years in the late seventies. I'd have nothing against the people now, but frankly it's not for me. There's something lacking."

"Well, they've no spirituality over there. I suppose it makes a difference that here, no matter who you are or where you come from, you meet up in the same place once a week."

"You're right there. I'd like my kids to grow up with some sort of culture, or traditions or something."

The voices seemed very far away from me, and yet I was part of it, it couldn't happen without me. Why did Tony have to mention children? I fastened my arms tight around me. The barman stole another long look and then continued, "There's no snobberies here anyway. Maybe the economy might be in a bad way, but the people who get to the top get there because they're good. Take the fella who opened this place, for example, Bobby Brennan. Took a massive gamble. Sweet-talked his bank manager into lending him enough to redo the place totally. Cost a fortune, everything's authentic. Well, the punters love it. Between yourself and myself there's very few pies in this city Bobby Brennan doesn't have a finger in now."

The door had begun to swing almost continuously, for it was five-thirty and wave after wave of people were converging on Brennan's as if they had made a secret arrangement. Their movements seemed as mechanical as genuflections in a church. What are they doing, I wondered, why don't they stop it? What is it makes them do this? I had no answer, but a face came into my mind, the face of a woman so beautiful that only the richest man in the world could have her for his own. Suddenly I realised that no-one would ever ask me to be more than an approximation to that face, that I would never get any thanks or appreciation for being anything else. And I felt giddy and sick, the voices slurred together, I couldn't stand it, the faces around me seemed completely foreign. Tony leant towards me saying something to me, but I put my hands to my ears. I thought I was going to faint and I slid off my stool and pushed through the people to the Ladies. Miraculously, there was no-one there, and I clicked on the latch. The silences and the white surfaces calmed me. I bent down and washed my face and then looked up at myself. I had never been more struck by my beauty. My eyes were like sapphire against the soft bronze of my skin, and my hair hung round me in a great gold mass. I could hear Tony knocking at the door but I ignored him. I started to smile and the face in the mirror smiled and nobody else could see it, only me. Nobody else could have it. This was what I wanted then, I thought, and I felt happy for the first time since my marriage. Tony was trying to force the door but I pushed my back against it and I could see my strength reflected in the face in the mirror. I could hear lots of voices, and Tony's voice above them all, but I was smiling, and I didn't let them in.

And later when I miscarried and Tony came to see me I kept my eyes and my mouth shut.

I must hurry this now. I must close my book and wait for the nurse to bring in my tea. The Angelus sounds and the nuns and nurses shuffle through the long corridors. The Virgin's face is calm.

Concubine

People often ask me how I came to paint my masterpiece, the face of a woman on tobacco-gold silk. It has the look of the Turin shroud, ancient, archetypal. The expression on the woman's face is strong. It is proud. And it is mature. The face is my own. I painted it one strange morning, I painted it when I was drunk and ill and hallucinating. I am a successful painter, but this screen, which marks the beginning of a new phase, is the greatest thing I have ever done. I will never part with it. I signifies an important moment in my life, when I saw myself as I wish always to see myself. There is a story behind it.

Ten years ago; I was forty-five. I had moved into a new flat and I wanted everything perfect. I was painting again, after a long lapse. It was the start of a new life. A new me. I bought all the right materials. I painted the walls white. I set out my array of chinoiserie, the vase, the fans, the jade figurines my husband had brought me back from Hong Kong. I was painting a silk screen for each of the walls, one aqua, one red, one blue, one tobacco-gold. I was taking the patterns from the jade figurines, a lion, a horse, a dragon. I had one yet to paint, tobacco-gold and stretched tight on its frame. It was the largest figure, a beautiful Chinese woman, her dress elegant, her smooth face calm and smiling.

My husband had left me for a younger woman. It sounds banal, but the suffering, the dull pain, nails broken clutching my fists. The suffering. I wanted everything perfect. I ran hither and thither to find the right furnishings. I was exhausted all the time. And my paintings were awful. There was no breeze, no magic. Chinoiserie. I was exhausted. My husband had left me for a younger woman, and so I started to paint. I spent seventy-five pounds on make-up and cosmetics. I spent hours daubing myself. I knew each wrinkle intimately. I looked at myself from all angles. I saw no beauty there, which is perhaps why I found no beauty with my brush. I hated myself. I looked much worse than I had before. I kept trying to remember what I'd been like before and trying to find it. I could find it nowhere. I spent fifty pounds at the hairdresser and I spent a hundred pounds at the boutique. I didn't have that kind of money. But I spent it anyhow.

Everything I put on looked wrong. It looked too young or it looked too frumpy. I didn't blame him. I had expected it. I had almost willed him to it. I'd hated myself and I'd willed him to it. Once the children had got older, I'd lost my way. I'd lost all sense of myself. And I lost him. And yet it may not have been such a bad thing. But that was later. That was after the strangest night. I was drinking and doing sketches of the woman figurine. Half the whiskey was gone and I had a headache dinging in me. It must have been past midnight. The drawings were dead as doornails. I hated that figurine, I hated the whole idea. I hated my new flat. I hated myself. I took another drink and I tried to see the figurine in a new way. And suddenly as I stared it grew tall and bright. I saw her before me. Her face was white and smooth. Her hair was black, swept up into a great white head-dress. And her gown was white and red, the deepest red I have ever seen. Her black eyes sparkled. I knew I had had a lot to drink, and so I closed my eyes. Then I opened them. And she was still there. I asked her what her name was and she said "Sang-Fei-Kwei." I asked her who she was and she said, "I was one of the emperor's concubines. I was a concubine of Yung-Lo."

I nodded, because I knew little of Chinese history, and I could understand nothing of what was happening. I just knew she sat before me in colours so strident I could not doubt them. I sat back and she started to speak. "I made that figurine. It's an image of myself. Carving was what I was good at. Everybody needs that, something they can do or make—just for themselves. I had no learning like you, but as long as I had my carving I was contented, and people respected me."

"Where did you come from?" I asked.

"From you," she said simply. I shook my head.

Then she said, "You feel worthless, don't you?"

I nodded.

She leaned forward and said, "I was worthless. I was given to the emperor when I was nine years old. I come from a rich family, but they had fallen on hard times. They couldn't afford a dowry, they couldn't even afford to keep me. I was beautiful. He started at me then. Later they told me that was why I never had children. I became his favourite. I was very intelligent and I knew how to play him along. I knew what to do for him."

She laughed coquettishly. Bitterly.

"No wonder I was his favourite. Oh yes, there was his wife, there were other concubines. The harem was full. But he liked me best. And my power was limitless. I had private quarters, I had a bathing-pool, a peacock..."

I grew restless and she felt my irritation. She leant close.

"I made the best of my situation. What choice did I have? I had no learning. The emperor liked us innocent as song-birds. I couldn't read or write and I was the most powerful woman in China. I let nothing beat me. Except time. I thought nothing of it, but the years rolled on. I thought nothing of it. It was almost imperceptible at first. I began to be sent for a little less. Then a little less again. I had a eunuch as my special attendant and I asked him, 'Why doesn't the emperor call for me?' 'The emperor is busy,' that's all he said. But of course, everyone was small-minded in that place. No-one had any dignity. And I was uppity. And nervy. One day my eunuch spilt a drop of wine in my face-paste and I shouted,

'Can't you be more careful?'

'It was just a bit of wine!'

'Don't be insolent!'

'I'm not insolent!'

'I'll have the emperor speak to you.'

'When did you last see the emperor?'

I looked up. 'I saw him yesterday.'

'You didn't.'

'I did!'

'He was with the young girl last night.'

'The young girl?'

'From Hangchow.'

He was relenting, for he loved me dearly, as I loved him. There were tears running through my make-up and he came to me and stroked my hair. I said, 'Does the emperor send you no word for me?'

He hated the emperor and he wouldn't lie to me. He said, 'The emperor says you're an old woman now.'

I turned away from him and wept. He kissed my hair and we sat deep in our own sadnesses for most of the night.

I hoped for a while, but the emperor never called me again. I was bitter at first. I was just thirty-five, imagine! And the emperor was sixty-eight! I gave myself up to weeping and face-painting. There were orders that I be kept comfortable, but my eunuch died from slow poison in his wound, and his replacement was careless and rude. My room was full of dirt and empty jugs, for I drank myself to sleep most nights. I gambled with the old harlots who little by little came to share my space. I was still beautiful and I loved to see the envy on their faces. And sometimes I slept with them, just to have someone touch me and call me beautiful."

"It was your own fault," I said angrily, angry that she should have woken my pain.

"I had no choice," she said. "Not like you. And look what you did. Sold yourself. A thousand years and you've learnt nothing. You set yourself up in a little empire, with its own harem. All those breakfasts in bed and sprigs of parsley and French knickers! You deserve to feel as you do. No-one has the right to make anyone else responsible for her own self-esteem."

"So what happened to you in the end?" I asked vindictively.

Sang-Kwei-Fei smiled. "I began to carve. I turned my talent for dress and my imagination in love-making into shapes in jade. At first I carved chess-men—we all did, it was an imperial commission. But it was soon obvious I was talented, and I began to let my originality run through me to create something uniquely mine." She smiled again. "My figurines became much in vogue, though probably most people thought it was a man who made them. I set myself up, eventually, in a private house." She laughed. "I took a young lover. He hadn't a penny. But he respected me." She smiled. After a moment, she seemed to rouse herself. "Now, Anna," she said, "shouldn't you paint me as I am, from your imagination, not from a figurine?"

I knew the inspiration would not last and so I rushed to paint. With each brush-stroke she dissolved into air until I was alone in my flat in the early morning, with my brush and my tobacco-gold silk. And I don't know how it was, but the image on the silk was that of my own face. Strong. Proud. And mature.

Miracles

D eirdre slammed the door shut and relaxed against it a minute, and suddenly she found she was crying. She got herself into the sitting-room and sat down, let her eye run over the wedding photo, the photos of the kids. Going to the pictures on Francis Street, kissing in the Phoenix Park. What a lovely man he was then, so gentle, so considerate. They'd fallen in love and got married early, had children early. They'd been squashed into a tiny house, but they'd managed. There was always a little extra for a drink or a hairdo. Then this redundancy... At first she'd been brave. He's skilled, she'd thought, he'll find work. Two months had gone by, then three. The electric kettle broke, Patrick had his first communion. Her hair... The weather getting colder, and her trudging along to the Health Centre in her summer shoes.

Had she begun to resent him? Pointless to deny it. She'd let herself go. She looked a fright. There you are, look what you've done, she was saying. Was it any wonder he'd gone as bad as he had. He'd stopped looking for work, started drinking. He'd lost all his dignity. She'd hated him then. She'd crisped rigid in the bed, made sure he didn't touch her. They'd started shouting at each other, "Jesus woman, you look like me old mother."

"What's the use of keepin' myself nice if we never go out?" She'd thought her love for Eoin was strong enough not to be affected by poverty, but she'd learned different.

She'd been counting on the Christmas bonus to buy presents for the three boys and food for the holiday. She should have put in for a separate payment but she couldn't find it in herself to do that to Eoin. She'd sat at home waiting, and time had gone by. He'd only had thirty pounds on him when he got in. She'd screamed at him then, "They're your children too, you know." He'd just grunted at her and gone to sleep. She'd walked all over the house, the nerves standing up on her neck, muttering, "What am I going to do?" If only she could rid herself of Eoin, there might be a chance she could cope. If only she could rid herself of the coughing, peeing monster she had in the house. If she had some time to herself, she could manage. If she had some peace.

It was then she'd thought of Eoin's sister out in Tallaght. They had plenty of space out there, plenty of money. She went downstairs and rang Orna and to her embarrassment she cried again on the phone. "I just need some time alone, Orna. We're at each other's throats all day. We'll murder each other if we're together over the holiday."

Miraculously, Orna understood. Eoin's eyes were open now and Deirdre calculated and said, "If only I could get you out of the house for Christmas I'd get a little peace."

He rose to it, as she thought he would. "I might just go now. I just might."

"What about going to Orna's."

"I wouldn't mind going up there where everything's nice and cosy, and there's a bit of respect shown."

And so Orna collected him and promised to bring the kids up to see him soon. He'd left with the last of the money, and Deirdre'd been too proud to ask Orna for any. She had to get some money somewhere. And so the next day she put on her coat and told the older boys to look after Patrick. She went blindly into pubs and cafes, asking them if they needed extra help for the Christmas. They looked at her, bemused. She was only twenty-eight, but she had that blanched look only poor mothers have. Most people were kind, but there was no work, it was all given out already to fleet-footed seventeen-year-olds.

Then one of the fast-food waitresses stopped her at the door and said, "Yer man Ben out there selling the Christmas trees wants someone to sell up the way." And so Deirdre went out and tried.

"What age are you?" he asked brusquely, and she said, "Twenty-four."

"Have you any selling experience?"

She had. She had worked in Woolworth's. It was hardly relevant. But the people kept rushing by, some perhaps still without trees, workaholics leaving it till the last minute.

"O.K., " he said. "Ten quid a day."

He loaded his hand-cart with some trees and pulled them up the road. And so they began to sell, and every few hours they'd have to high-tail it down a laneway between the houses when the guards came on the scene.

The next day Deirdre got the kids dressed up as well as she could manage, and Orna came to bring them up to see their Dad. They were excited, knowing there were food and presents ahead of them, knowing Orna and Liam would do them proud. Deirdre was back selling trees by ten and the trade was brisker now. She got very cold, but she kept her mind on the collection of stiff, pink notes she was making. Things were going well for Ben; he brought her for a drink at seven. It was almost exciting to sit there after a day's work, without the dread that she had of pubs when Eoin was around. He offered her a second drink, but she didn't take it, she went home and filled hot-water bottles for the kids. Orna brought them home clutching their presents and pressed a tenner into Deirdre's hand as she was leaving. Deirdre hugged her until they both had tears in their eyes.

"How's Dad?" she asked the children as casually as she could.

"He's grand, " Hugh said, and Jim added, "Why wouldn't he be? All he has to do is sit by the fire all day and have his food brought to him." Hugh and Jim sided with their mother. But little Patrick still kept his loyalty to his Dad. "He dressed up as Santa. He gave us each a packet of sweets."

And so it was Christmas Eve. Deirdre thought Ben would never shut up shop. He was determined to get rid of as many trees as possible. At eight o'clock she begged him to let her leave her trees with him and go. He gave her an extra fiver and promised to drop a tree up to the house on the way home. She went quickly to the late-night supermarket and bought the usuals, bread, milk, tea, but also a large chicken, vegetables, a tin of biscuits, a chocolate cake, some holly and a few hanging Santas for the tree. She bought the boys a selection box each, and some nicknack, toy cars, a small teddy. It was as she left the shop swinging her plastic bags that she noticed a strange feeling had come over her and she wondered what it was. Was it...Yes, she was happy. She was happy. She got home with her bulging parcels, and Jim and Hugh had Patrick in his pyjamas. Then she sat down and looked at them straight and said, "Listen kids. There's no such thing as Santa. Dadda and I used to fill the stockings."

Jim and Hugh looked at her gently. They had known, of course. Only little Patrick was wide-eyed, disbelieving. "How come Johnny Maher said he saw him, then?"

"Johnny Maher must have been dreaming. Mr. Maher fills his stocking, the same as I did yours. But this year Dadda's unemployed...and he's not well. There just isn't the money. Hang up your stockings like you always do, an' there'll be some surprises for you in the morning. But nothing like you got last year when Dadda was workin' an' things were different."

"Is it going to go on like this, Ma?" said the eldest, "Or what's going to happen?"

"It's not going to go on like this. I think Dadda and I are going to take some time apart. I'm going to get my dole separately. And if you and Hugh can look after Patrick after school, I think I'm going to get some kind of a job."

She felt strong and satisfied and Hugh smiled at her. She was so glad she'd told them straight. So many people borrowing from money-lenders and putting themselves into debt, just to keep their children believing in Santa. Her children would know what was what. They wouldn't expect more than was reasonable. Only little Patrick remained unconvinced, and he said as he was going to bed. "I think Santa'll come anyway, no matter what you say."

About ten o'clock Deirdre and Jim were decorating the tree when the phone rang. It was Mary, Deirdre's friend who lived nearby. Her husband worked in America and couldn't get home this Christmas. "Can we come over and spend Christmas with you and we'll put our food together?" she asked. Deirdre was delighted. Everything was turning out so well.

The next morning the children opened their stockings, and the way they went on you'd think they'd got bicycles and electric trains. Maybe Jim and Hugh were putting it on for her sake. They did tell her that Patrick expected Santa to pay a surprise visit during the day and confound them all. There were one or two curious looks at Mass, because Eoin wasn't there, but more people understood, patted Deirdre on the shoulder, patted the children on the head.

Then Maria came round and they lit a fire and roasted the two big chickens. Maria had brought loads of food, chocolates, a plum-pudding, a cake. Her children came carrying the portable TV between them. She and Deirdre tippled at a bottle of red wine and a bottle of whiskey, and before long Deirdre felt merry. She was serving up the best meal the children had seen in six months, and the children were laughing, playing with Mary's children. The Christmas tree sparkled and Deirdre put Bing Crosby on the record player. Soon enough there was pudding, and then cake and coffee. The children put on the TV and watched a film, while Maria and Deirdre relaxed and had a really good talk. Then the phone rang and it was Orna. Deirdre worried for a moment, but everything was going fine there, the neighbours' children were in and Eoin was keeping them all amused with his jokes. Everything was working out beautifully. He wanted to speak to the children, of course, and so Hugh and Jim very distantly did their turns. Then little Patrick. "He didn't come yet…Mam says he's not…I told her he would…I am, Dad, I am keepin' a look-out…"

He rang off and everyone relaxed again, until it was ten o'clock and Maria picked up her youngest child, who was asleep, kissed Deirdre goodbye and walked home. Deirdre sat on the couch with Patrick on her knee, and the eldest two watched TV. The fire was dying but the room was still warm. And she felt warm inside too. The terrible thing was to be at the mercy of someone else's temper. If she could get a bit of independence, there was no telling what she might do. Christmas had turned out so well this year, and she had been dreading it. She could face the New Year with confidence. There was no telling what miracle could happen. Anything was possible.

Patrick's eyes grew round, suddenly, and he sat up. There was a rush of wind and Hugh and Jim looked away from the television. Jim stretched out his finger and Deirdre looked too. There was a white-bearded man standing in the sitting-room in a red suit, a red hat, black boots and a black belt. Father Christmas was standing in the sitting-room. The back door, the yard door, stood magically open behind him. He was smiling. He came forward. Deirdre tried to hold Patrick back, but he wriggled off her knee and went for the sack that Santa held beside him. Jim, Hugh, Deirdre stared. Patrick dived in. He felt around for a few moments, then looked puzzled. "Why is there nothing there, Santa?" he asked, wide-eyed.

Santa said, "Ho-ho-ho!" and took off his hat. "You're a pack of eejits. I was havin' you on. Orna's parkin' the car, she'll be in any minute."

And Eoin lifted the tearful Patrick up in his arms and said, "Didn't I tell you Santa'd come, Pat. And wasn't I right?"

Queensland

For James

It was incredible he had got that far. I heard this shuffling in the store and I thought it was a rat, or maybe an Aborigine stealing our carefully stacked bags of government flour. But I wasn't frightened.

"Who's there?" I called. There was no answer, but I waited, I stood perfectly still. And then I heard it again. I approached the flour sacks. I could hear breathing now, getting quicker, stronger. I approached steadily, a strange reaction for a young, unarmed woman, but I wasn't frightened of the Aborigines and they trusted me. "Don't be afraid," I said, "Come out!" Suddenly something sprang at me, I felt, I smelt a man. We fell to the floor and I screamed for help and then the strangest thing happened; he went weak all at once. He fell off me onto his face and began to cry like a child. And to my amazement he said, "Christ help me, Christ help me," and so he was a white. It was incredible he had got that far. I said, "Ssh!" and tried to calm him. I reached out to touch him but he was rigid with terror, he winced from my fingers. He wouldn't stop crying then, but I never saw him cry again. He never referred to those first moments and I really think he forgot them.

I guessed he was an escaped convict. Rumours of

them were always coming to our small outback mission station. I believed in justice certainly, but I had seen things at the penal settlements that had shocked me. I felt sorry for this poor specimen of an escapee, and it was my instinct to protect him. He was in a terrible state; he was so thin I found it hard to look at him. But I knew I had to get him clean for risk of infection and as I worked I justified and planned. I reckoned he was too ill to go back and be tried and punished again, and I decided to harbour him until he was well and I was quite sure I was sending him to justice and not to death. He was very modest and made me turn while he took off his bits of trousers. All the time he kept up a low pleading patter in a comical accent I recognised as an Irish brogue, "Missus, they put me in chains an' made me work twelve hours in the splitting sun Missus, an' never fed me, Missus, an' one time I sung a rebel song an' they flogged me, they gave me a hundred lashes o' the cat." It was just then I was frightened of what I might see, festering weals and half-decayed flesh. But his back was clear, the beautiful, smooth back of a young man. I said nothing but I became confused and doubtful. I got him some of Henry's old clothes and some milk-sopped bread, the only food mild enough for a man that sick.

James, he said his name was and I told him mine was Ruth. He was about twenty-five or twenty-six it seemed, with hair like dark hay and dull grey eyes. No-one could have called him handsome, but his face fascinated. No mood settled on it for more than a few moments. I made him a comfortable bed behind the grain sacks and he lay down. He kept apologising, I had to raise my voice to make him stop. I cleaned him again and left him some milk and then went out and began my work so as not to cause suspicion. But when I passed the store later in the day, I found the door slightly open. I was afraid he had left and wandered back into the bush, or that Henry had gone in and found him. I rushed inside, but there was James, standing alone in the square of light. "Do you want to get caught?" I said.

"I'm sorry Missus," said James, "but I was lonely and I didn't like the dark."

"You know they'll send you to Norfolk Island if they catch you. You're much too sick to go."

"Sure who'd catch me here, anyway?"

"My husband would."

In fact I didn't know how Henry would react. It had seemed to me recently that he considered his divine calling as much a duty to the government as to God.

"You'll send me off yourself once I'm well, anyway," said James.

"You won't stand a chance if you go back now."

"I don't want to stay in the dark alone. It makes me think o' solitary."

"I'll have to tell my husband then. You can explain yourself to him."

"Listen Missus," he said. "I'm no convict at all. I've just got into the habit of saying that."

The lie was pathetic, I thought. There was no reason for a free man to set off alone into the Queensland bush. "Don't lie to me," I said.

"Listen," said James. "I'm a free man, not a convict. I have me ticket of leave." He began rustling in his discarded trousers, and I waited for the excuses, I lost it, you took it. Then he held forward a piece of paper and I read it. He had been free for two years. I couldn't say anything for a moment. I didn't understand.

I said, "It's suicide to go into the bush alone. If you hadn't found this place, God knows what would have happened to you." Then a thought came to me. "Did you commit another crime?"

"I committed no crime, Missus." James was pleased with the effect he had produced.

"Then what happened?" I insisted.

"Can't you wait till I get my breath?"

I remembered his weakened state and began gathering up his things to bring him inside. I was relieved that now I could be reasonably sure of his recovery. James was acting as jauntily as his condition permitted. I set him up by the fire and he leaned back and took in the scene, delighted with himself. Then I asked again, "Why did you come out into the bush alone?"

"I couldn't sleep," he said, "and I thought I'd take a walk until sleep came to me."

I waited for him to smile or laugh but he did neither. I was tired of his lies and tired of struggling. I looked him in the face and said "I see." But his eyes were closing and his head was falling back.

II

It's odd that when I want to write about my husband's death, I always start with James's coming and the strangeness of that Australian spring, as if they were connected in some way. It was 1859 and I was twenty-three years old, I had been in Australia nine months.

Henry was forty-five and in fact I had first met him as a schoolgirl when he came to prepare my class for confirmation. He was handsome and dynamic and I think almost the whole class wanted to marry him. But I was the one he chose. Henry went away to Australia for a few years after that, and then one day he appeared on the doorstep, tanned and more handsome than ever. It was soon obvious to everyone that I was being courted. I was out of my mind with joy. Henry had such exciting plans. He wanted to go back to Australia and work among the Aborigines, bringing them to civilisation and then to God. He needed a woman to help him, and I was ready. And that was how I came to be teaching English to the Barunda tribe in the Queensland bush. Religious instruction could not get very far until the natives had a grasp of English, as Henry knew nothing of the native tongue. But I soon picked up a basis of common words, and though I'm sure I sounded ridiculous, it meant I could talk to an old person or comfort a small child.

Henry said I was slowing down the learning process, that Aboriginal languages had no equivalent words for truth, justice or even God, and should be abandoned as far as possible. I couldn't argue back because my knowledge of the language was too sparse. But the fact remained that I was accepted and Henry was not. We were assigned two English convicts, Tom and Billy, and we treated them well. We cleared some bush and built our little station, a small house and store, and a school-room which doubled as a church. We had studied the Barundas' migratory habits, and we built beside their winter camp. We chose the Barunda because they had had little contact with the whites so far, and were thus open and welcoming... "uncontaminated" was the word we used. We gained their friendship through our gifts of flour, tobacco, shelter and medical care. And in exchange they attended school, chanting English phrases for a time each afternoon. They spoke several Aboriginal languages already, and in fact during peaceful negotiations with other tribes, Aboriginal spokesmen swapped languages. Perhaps it was this openness that made them so quick to learn English. I was astonished at their progress.

We had not succeeded in becoming self-sufficient. We cleared and cultivated, but the earth was dry and unyielding. Our pitiful handful of livestock gave us milk and some wool, and it was our great boast that the cow was pregnant, but we knew the animals would not be replaced by the government, and so we slaughtered none. We nibbled nervously at the flour and salt meat we had brought with us, we fished, and we hoped for better weather and more regular help from the natives. They would have to change their ways if the farm expanded as our livestock would displace their wild game. They would face starvation if they didn't. But we hoped the change would come as naturally as a change in the season, and that everyone would benefit in the end.

I truly wanted that. As my knowledge of the Barundas' language improved, I grew more interested in their culture, and I began to understand the importance of the land to them. They had no God as we understand the word. But for thousands of years they had lived and died on that land, so that rocks, trees, rivers, were incandescent with meaning for them. Their tracks were changeless so that past and present fused, and time stayed still. I saw it would be the end of them if they did not fully share in what we did with the land. They were so sure of their title to it that they saw no harm in our settling. To them we were just a moment in the flow of time. We brought them benefits and they did not fear us. We treated them well and were well treated in return. But I was uneasy. I could read the signs. I heard about the killings, the poisonings, the rapes, and I felt a net closing around us. I was thankful the Barunda had heard very little, and seeing us as a separate tribe, did not in any case associate us with the atrocities. People said our race was killing theirs, infecting them with diseases they could not fight off, starving them by scattering the game and weeding out the edible roots. Some said it was inevitable, some that it was God-ordained. And one Archbishop said it would be a blessing when the last one finally went under.

And so I was jumpy and sensitive and some of Henry's attitudes annoyed me. He felt that the missionary work was being held up by my inadequacy as an English teacher. He said I was too slow and gentle, I spent more time learning their language than teaching them mine. I began to realise that there were irreconcilable differences between us. I had been very immature when I married him. No doubt I would have remained contented had we stayed in England. But the experience of Australia had beaten me down and sculpted me into an individual. Here there was little comfort and scant cleanliness, no niceties and no society. You had to sift your experience for the things that make life bearable. But Henry had not opened up to it, he had clenched tight against the bush. He threw himself into fighting back the wilderness and the silence, and the effort left him exhausted and ill-tempered. And these fissures were shaking open when that sick young Irishman stumbled out of nowhere.

III

He came from Dublin city, he said. He slept for a couple of hours that afternoon and woke in time to share our supper. Henry was full of concern for the man, and was, I suspect, hopeful he might be converted from Catholicism and kept on as a desperately needed labourer. As usual, Henry went to bed early, drained from his day of manual work, but I stayed up as I often did, writing letters, writing my journal. I kept the lamp on my table burning low so as not to disturb James, whose eyes had closed again, whose motionless body the fading embers etched. Perhaps an hour passed like that, the tick of the clock the only sound. I leaned over James to put the guard on the fire in case it spat at him during the night. Suddenly, his hand clutched mine. "Missus," he said, "are you taking away the light?"

"You frightened me. I thought you were still asleep," I said.

"I stayed still like that because I didn't want you to stop."

"You'd better go to sleep now. You need to get up your strength."

"I can't sleep these nights, whatever it is."

"What do you mean?"

"I can't shut my eyes. I'm weak with it. I can't sleep these nights at all."

Like a fool I asked, "Would you like a little brandy to calm you?" and he accepted. He drank with pleasure, but he showed no signs of sleeping. "What did you do that they sent you out here?" I asked suddenly.

"Ah now," he said with wilful mysteriousness, "that's a long story. Before I was even born I had everything taken from me. I never had anything to lose."

"Were you involved in politics?"

"I was."

"And you were given seven years?"

"Yes."

I couldn't help feeling a certain admiration for him. I barely remembered the last Irish rebellion, but rebel memories were alive among the Irish convicts, I had seen the texts of some rebel songs. Of course, I thought they were wrong, but provoked by the greater wrong of British policy. This poor young man, I thought, wrenched from everything and everyone he knew. The tragedy of it was endless and mute as the endless acres of blue Pacific he had crossed.

I left the lamp, it blazed away under the door all night. Days passed and things fell into a pattern, Henry going to bed, the lamp, the talk. James was no better, in fact he seemed to be weakening. He stayed awake all night and slipped into a drunken doze for a couple of hours in the early morning. I began to understand how disturbed he was. Henry was getting restless with the whole situation. James was another mouth to feed, after all, and he was showing no signs of being strong enough to work.

What little energy he had he used talking. I began to rely on him for my entertainment, I left my writing and reading aside.

"We were lying on the dark hill waiting for the signal. The house was dark, but we were waiting, watching. The timing had to be right, you see. We weren't speaking but we were all excited. If it went right we'd get them back for a lot. We waited. I was beginning to think maybe something'd happened to him, but then it came, the light. And we ran, dead silent, over the grass and there was the crash of breaking glass, and it'd begun...

He would look round anxiously for the brandy and I would give it to him to make him go on, "God, I remember the blaze of it! We had them standing in their night-clothes on the gravel in the end. It was nothing like an eviction, maybe...but still, it was good. And then we vanished into the night. We just vanished..."

It always seemed to me he was leaving something out. I asked him how he was arrested.

"Some damn talker, of course. They had us up in court. I was only showing them justice, you know. I know what's right and what's wrong."

"Did you have to turn to violence?"

"Hadn't we tried talking? They won't listen. They only understand violence, Missus." And then he'd say, "You'll leave the lamp tonight, won't you?"

I wondered how he could rely on us so much. We were English, after all. But the bush changed all that, the bush was the common enemy. And the weather began to get hot, the work harder. Henry started grumbling openly about James, and I suggested he start working a bit. His tired eyes stared in his pale face when I said it, but he went meekly. He napped under a tree with the men at noon, but the work gave him no ease at night, the talk continued, the lamp stayed lit. It was worrying to see him wide awake while Henry snored next door, and to think that they had worked together during the day. And the brandy went down in the bottle and James told and retold his stories, his eyes fixed all the time on something unforgettable which he couldn't tell.

IV

The temperature soared and now every night we heard singing from the Aborigines' camp. I asked a young woman why and she said they were chasing away the winter. At the time I laughed. It seemed wonderfully self-deceptive to attribute the change of the seasons to one's own magic powers. But then I began to envy the equal partnership these people had with nature. They neither dominated nor idealised, they struck a balance.

It saddened me then when an old man told me the tribe would leave when summer came. I wasn't sure if he was right, of course, I hoped he was mistaken. If they left it would make the mission a mere winter shelter for the Aborigines, a convenient stop-over, and I couldn't yet bear to think in those terms. And I didn't like to think what it might do to Henry. He was unhappy as it was. The temperature soared and he hated it, he wouldn't sink back into it. He battled. He threw himself into furious activity. He stepped up his programme of religious instruction. But although he had been inspiring as a clergyman in London, he was not a good enough communicator to cut through thousands of years of conditioning and civilisation, not to mention a language barrier. He blamed the language barrier on me, he said my foolish attempts to learn the language had weakened my teaching. The bush was tearing us apart and we seemed to speak to each other very little.

James caused stress between us, but I didn't want him to leave, he filled some sort of imaginative need in me. The world of his stories lived side by side with the real world for me now, and Henry could not share in it. I had grown fond of James; I loved his quaint expressions, his strange accent, his changeable face. I knew that his talk was a defence against darkness, and that once he understood the darkness, he would sleep peacefully. It pained me to see him mount his defence of words as darkness fell. But I would have been disappointed if he had turned over and gone to sleep, and left me to my books and my silence.

And so things were falling apart and I wasn't holding them together as I suppose I should have been. And then the night came when everything changed. James was sitting in the corner mending his shoes and I was cooking, when Henry came in, exhausted from his religious instruction class. I put his food down in front of him and asked how it had gone. "Nowhere," he said.

I tried to encourage him, "They come anyway. They sit and listen quietly."

"They do that because of what we give them. They

have no intention of converting, Ruth."

"Given time you never know what might happen."

"No, it's too late. Everyone's agreed there's only one thing to do. Take the children away from the parents and raise them separately."

"You can't do that!" The words were out before I knew it.

He seemed surprised, even amused. "It's no different from boarding school at home. We'd build a nice, clean little school here and look after them. We'd give them plenty of eat, clothes, medical care and a chance to make something of themselves"

"How could you justify taking children away from their parents?"

"I'd justify it by winning them for Christianity and civilisation."

"Parents have a natural right to take charge of their children's education."

"Education? Is that what they get from their parents?"

"Formation, then."

"The parents would be more than glad to resign the responsibility."

"Only if they're desperate. Only if they see no other hope for their children!"

It was then I noticed we were shouting. I was horrified for a few seconds and then I began to enjoy it. I realised I had wanted to shout at Henry for some time. The realisation passed between us and we went on with new freedom, "What do you want for the Aborigines, Ruth? Do you want them to be Christianised?"

"Of course I do. I just think they have to come to it

naturally, of their own accord. I don't think we should kill their culture and force them to take on ours."

"Our civilisation is Christian civilisation, and in that it is superior to theirs. We have a moral duty to spread that civilisation."

I knew Henry had logic on his side, but I struck out anyway, "If you force your civilisation on theirs, you'll destroy them. Just as you'll destroy them if you take their land."

"Certain aspects of their culture need destroying. If they've a child too many and they want to move on—what do they do? Bash out its brains in the bush!"

"We're killers too, Henry. We're killing them."

Drums and singing started in the background, and we both felt it reinforced our case.

I said, "We could learn from them if we listened."

"About the land, yes. But as far as religion goes, we have everything to teach them."

"Religion and land are one and the same thing for them."

"By extension then, you'd have us learning from their religion?"

"Why not?"

I had a vague feeling I had said something crucial. Henry's face struggled between anger and amazement, and anger won. He moved stiffly to the bedroom and shut the door, the bed creaked once. I went stiffly to the bookcase and took down a novel. Then I looked over at James and he smiled at me mischievously.

"I'm sorry to put you through all that," I said.

"He'll have me turned into a Protestant before I know where I am. I'll be dragged into his 'boarding school' and 'given a chance.' "

The smile faded then and I saw his strained face, "I wish they'd stop that desperate noise," he said, "I'm so tired."

"Would you sleep if I put out the lamp?"

"Not with that desperate noise, anyway."

He lay down on his bed. I opened my novel, but I couldn't read, I listened to the voices outside and all at once I understood: they would leave the next day. Perhaps I had heard a word, or perhaps I was just enough in tune with their culture to interpret. I felt a great, inevitable sadness.

"Are you asleep, James?" I said.

"No. Why?"

"Talk to me."

"Talk to me, you. I'm always telling the stories."

"I don't know what we're doing! I don't know how it all happened."

I moved to the chair beside James's bed, the one furthest from the bedroom door and Henry.

"I had such different expectations. I was so unsure of myself when I came out here. But we're doing more harm than good, James, aren't we?"

"Ah, don't worry," said James half-heartedly.

"Now I don't even know why we're here. I swear I don't." A new thought came to me. "Why don't you go back to Ireland? You're free now. You could get married, root yourself again. You could start again."

James looked at me pityingly. "No-one ever starts again in Ireland."

"I don't think the mission has much future, James," I said. "What's to become of you? Will you go back to Brisbane?"

"No. I'll go further inland. Further and further."

The Aborigines' voices were strong on the air, and the night seemed to grow hotter. I think we were affected by their ceremonies of parting, ending. I was asking things I had wanted to ask for a month, and James was sitting up, his eyes wide, hunted. "It's as if you're running away from something. The dark frightens you, you can't sleep at night." He was silent.

"Is it some crime you committed. Did you kill someone? I know it was a political act, but that needn't stop you from feeling guilty."

"Ah, would you stop talking nonsense. I never killed anyone."

"Did your companions kill someone then?"

"No, they didn't."

"So it was a peaceful political movement, was it? You're not telling the truth. You always tell me the high points of the rising, but the fact is, it failed. You never tell me how it was in the end. And no-one ever gets killed. You're always leaving something out. I think it's that that disturbs you and stops you from sleeping."

"Ah, you know everything about me, don't you Missus?" He glowered at me for a moment and then said, "I was never in any political movement. I was sent out here for killing a sheep."

"...You told me..."

"Ah, it was all lies."

"For killing a sheep?"

"I was starving. I thought I was going to die. Half of us on the island had died already, and the rest of us crawled round in the filth looking for roots, waiting for the Quaker soup. I'm from Clare Island, not

Dublin. You should have known that from my way of speaking. I never spoke a word of English at home. Well, anyway, I was sunk that low I stole a sheep and I killed it."

"When?"

"I was around sixteen. My mother and one of my sisters died of famine fever. It's a wonder I didn't go too. My father was dead already."

I had brought on this confession with my stupid questions. I leant forward and took his hand, but he went on, "I was glad they'd died. That way I had more food. I ate my fill and when they sentenced me to transportation I was glad. I would never have to look at that place again. I would never have to look at my neighbours or what was left of my family again. There was no-one else from the island on the boat, so I let on I was with the Young Irelanders. I nearly believe it myself now." He had said it all and nothing had happened. I still held his hand. His bitterness seemed to run out and he went weak. He looked at me wide-eyed. "Was I unnatural not to grieve after my mother and sister?"

"You can't blame yourself for anything?"

"I try not to think about them or to think about Ireland. I'm never going back."

We were silent for a moment, and then I realised what was strange. The voices and drums had stopped. "I think the Aborigines have gone, James," I said.

"How do you know?"

"I just feel it."

"What'll you do if they have?"

"I don't know." There was another silence. Then I

said, "I'm glad they're gone."

"But you... you got on grand with them from what I saw."

"For their sake, I mean. I'm glad they're gone."

Perhaps James didn't realise it, but this confession was as deep as his had been. He lay his sad, pale body back on the bed and closed his eyes. I felt a great ease come over me just to see him rest. I sat there in the great silence and my mind was blank. I must have slept a bit on the chair because the next thing I remember the morning was glowing blue through the window and James was standing in front of me, hoisting a bag onto his shoulder. I didn't ask where he was going. There was nothing left for him at the mission, anyway. It was useless to try and stop him, he had his track to follow, even if it led nowhere. He moved towards the door and smiled back at me, his face relaxed, his grey eyes warm. He said something in a voice I'd never heard before, soft, musical. I couldn't distinguish the words and I leaned forward. He repeated the phrase and then we both realised I would never understand it, I had never learned. The smile left his face, he raised his hand briefly and went out.

I got into bed beside Henry's sleeping body and rolled close to him. It was all over now and he was warm and human. But before I could fall asleep I felt him stirring, and then he was getting out of bed. I was powerless and closed my eyes and waited. Perhaps half an hour went by, and I was dipping into sleep, when Henry's voice called me back. "Ruth!"

I didn't want to open my eyes, and then I did, and I saw his empty face. All residue of anger left me. I got up and dressed and we went out together. The Aborigines' disappearance seemed magic in its completeness. Nothing remained except the smoking fire. No-one had come to say goodbye, no-one had left anything, not even the woman whose baby I had helped deliver two days before. But of course, that was only right. The season had changed and they had gone with it. I had given my help freely, as anyone would have done, and it had been freely accepted. There was nothing more to be said. I tried to catch Henry's hand, to find a reflection in his face. But when I looked at him his face seemed to close up against my eyes. "We'll find other people who need us, Henry," I said.

"No Ruth. We can't just let them wander off like that. We'll have to fetch them back." His voice was toneless. I wondered was he going out of his mind.

"We can't force them to stay."

"They need to be shown…"

"They have the right to make their own decisions."

"They need to be shown when they're making a mistake."

I couldn't stop him. The Queensland summer day was deep yellow when Henry set out with Billy and Tom. And the whole long day I sat inside on my own and tried to understand. I was frightened that Henry would find the Aborigines because I didn't know what he might do. There were a hundred of them, but Henry and his men had guns. And I worried too about my own safety alone in the creaky, echoing bush.

Late that night Henry and the men came home hungry and sun-struck. They hadn't even found a track. I thought that would be the end of it, but Henry wanted to go out again the next day. There were no words I could use against his determination. He and the men got up at dawn to tend to the animals, and then they went off. The day blued up. I wandered hopelessly about the house looking for something to do. It was late morning when I went into the yard and saw the open barn door. I felt sick to my stomach, I approached slowly and peered into the dark, hoping it was just that my eyes weren't used to it. But of course, the animals had gone. All of them. I stumbled round the edges of the clearing yelling out for them, but there was no sign, no sound of them. They can't have lasted long in the bush, poor transplanted features of the English countryside. The mission was finished now, there would not be enough food. I felt sure Henry had left the door open, and I suspected he wouldn't care.

I never knew exactly what happened in the bush that day, but Tom and Billy bolted anyway, and I never saw them again. The sun and the hunger were confusing Henry, but some terrible determination in him refused to give. I begged him not to leave me alone the next day. I wanted to rediscover the strength in our marriage and work from that towards a new life. But Henry was older than me, he was tired of finding new ways. By now the Barunda had become for him only a symbol of evasive success. If only he could track down those fleet dark bodies in the bush, his life would mean something to him. And so the next day, though I did everything short of raising a gun to stop him, he went out alone.

The sun burned through the clear sky and I sat in the dark house. By now I had learned not to jump at every stir in the trees. I had come into step with the bush. I didn't worry about the Aborigines, they were far away by now, not even the white man's horse could catch them. Now I worried about the white man himself, unprotected against the climate, and with only his own senseless determination to guide him. It began to get dark and the silence filled with echoes, James's voice, the songs and drums of the Aborigines. I sat beside the lamp, bringing my hands together and parting them, looking out into the darkness.

He was out in the sun too long, they said. He was as unprotected as anyone on the dry plains. He was all I had left, and he didn't know how to take care of himself. He didn't come home.

I stayed. I had changed too much ever to fit in again in the London society I had left. I set up as a teacher, I teach convicts' children, not Aborigines. They had too many teachers. I see them now, prostitutes and beggars, I hope to recognise no faces.

I never saw James again. I did all I could to trace him, but no-one had ever heard of him. Who knows what his real name was. I hope he forgave himself and went home. Or found some patch of innocent land he could give new names in his soft language.

The Landscape Painter

hear my mother's step now on the landing. She pauses a second to listen anxiously. I am in here all day, quite silent, you see. She is terrified for me, and cannot know I am more terrified for myself. I could never say that out loud. I consign that to soundless words. It used to be I spent the days reading, sitting on this chair. Thus the elegance of my style. I emulate the greatest teachers. There are few important intellectual movements I have not studied with some care. But I can not so easily re-shelve the books in my mind, and my erudition drives my mother mad. I feel the pressure in the house rising with each hour I spend locked in here, even now I feel it rising. I come down pale and late to tea and banish her arguments like a child blows dandelion seeds. "If ya don't mind"— that is her great rejoinder. If it hadn't been for the certainty of leaving "If ya don't mind" behind, she never could have persuaded me to go away.

Back again, back again, to my trip to the West last autumn. Why do I always end up by writing about that? It has no relevance. I have pulled the curtains over again, because I can no longer look out. It goes on and on and on, grey house after grey house after grey house. I say I will never look at anything else, I will force myself to make do. I say I don't see the point in anything else, that the grey road is an apt mirroring of my consciousness. But I weaken, and here I am again, weakening. I am writing again. I say I will not write, I will keep my eyes open on the horror of it all day. Yet here I am again in the dark, my hand flying along the page, flying off towards somewhere else.

If I gave you a picture and swore it was true. I walked down a winding path with her and the birds were making the most incredible noise. A dog stood up on a grass-covered wall and watched us in perfect silence, and the houses were low, smoking lazily, perfuming the air with turf smoke. All of a sudden we reached the strand, shaped by waves, by wind, the footprints scrupulously washed off it every day. It curved away from us like a perfect cuticle, shading from palest yellow to dark brown where the waves rippled—I can hear them washing now. Pieces of wood were flung carelessly here and there. Facing us was an island, and then peak after peak, probably for miles, all in varying shades of blue and grey. I kept expecting it to disappear, erupt, change. I expected it to disappoint me. No-one had made it, no human. And there was nothing to be said. It wasn't words, it was a picture, do you understand? Being something as opposed to getting somewhere. Not like this place, a string of expletives spewed from the mouth of some town planner. You would have had to be very trusting to live with that landscape. There would have had to be a lot of silence in your speech.

I could never have fitted in. And yet, to be truthful, I am not content with what I have here. There are times when I can't rejoice in this pain I have, a clenched fist in the pit of my stomach. There are times when I can't take such sweet satisfaction from saying, look at Dermot Mulligan, he's alone, he's miserable and he's still alive. It was really loneliness that drove me to join the Hunger Strike support campaign. I helped to organise a few marches, nothing much, but I had a few near misses with the police. The mother was hysterical, of course. I refused to tell her anything, save what she could glean from the passages of history I learned and recited, for her entertainment, at the tea-table. She gleaned little. She took me to a doctor, who referred me to a psychiatrist. I told them nothing. "I was a bit 'unhappy,'" said the latter eminent gentleman, "I needed a change." It was what she had been waiting for. The neighbours chipped in, and before I knew where I was, I was plummeting to Mrs Flanagan's guesthouse with dozens of clean socks and no books.

I remember the journey, my head against the cold window, wondering how she had persuaded me to go. Little by little, the bus dribbled people out to their waiting families. The rain closed in, beating against the panes. Eventually, there were only three locals left on the bus, chatting to the driver in indecipherable monotone. We lurched to a halt and I staggered out into darkness such as I had never experienced. I was directed across the road and I walked a lane towards a belt of tossing trees. Waves were crashing somewhere in the blackness. I reached the house and rang the bell, but there was no sound, and soon I resorted to rapping, bare-fisted, at the door. A dim light approached the glass and Mrs Flanagan appeared, her old face lit up cruelly by the candle she carried.

She had given me up, she said, had gone to bed. I noted her Dublin accent with surprise. I explained that the bus had taken a diversion because the sea had smashed the bridge wall and swept in over the road. She made use of the reference to the weather to excuse the lack of electricity. Whatever way the wiring was, she said, the lights always cut out in bad weather. We walked along the dark corridor, slatted by moonlight where the doors of the empty rooms stood open. I heard a noise, like a child's cry of fear and Mrs Flanagan faltered perceptibly. Then she ushered me into a room and pressed a key into my hand, barely muttering "goodnight" before hurrying back down the corridor. A door banged and the crying stopped. I shut the curtains over the face of the moon and got into bed, rolling into a ball, as is my custom. Yes, I was still the same shape, the same Dermot. No-one could take that away. I was determined that my mother see no change in me when I returned. There is no change.

Not even Niamh could change me. I remember how I met her the first morning. I was gazing over my grease-thick plate at a rare bit of sunlight on the strand, on the mountains. An old man sat by the door, a hat pulled down to his eyes, rolling his tongue round his toothless mouth. Something like fear came into his face when she entered, and he hurried into the kitchen. I remember she made to follow the old man but when she saw me, she stopped and walked over, an open smile on her face. I was astonished by that look of frank delight at the presence of another person. She was a short, stocky woman, with thick, black curls and uneven teeth which gave her a witchy appearance when she smiled. Her cheeks were flushed, as if she had been running in a cold wind. I tried to age her, but she was past the age when the years stand out separately like rings on a tree. Over thirty, I guessed. With incredible confidence she introduced herself and sat down. I lowered my face to avoid the look of intense interest in her startling green eyes. She questioned me insistently, smiling her crooked smile when I looked up to answer. She was a landscape painter, she said, but she ran a home-weaving business for the bread and butter. She was Mrs Flanagan's niece and she came here to help out and to paint. She turned and looked out the window where the sun was disappearing and the sea was dark and ominous. When she turned back again she found my eyes on her and she smiled widely.

She suggested she bring me down to the strand, and I saw no way of refusing. We walked along the winding path until it scattered into sand. She ran to the water's edge. I followed her at an even speed, and then to my amazement she took off her shoes and socks and began to splash along in the waves. I couldn't imagine how she stood the cold. She felt no need now to make conversation, she ran her feet through the water, smiling gently. She was as much at ease in silence as in speech. Finally I could stand it no longer, and for want of anything else, I asked her about the crying I had heard the night before.

"Maurice, you remember, the old man in the dining-room... He often has bad dreams."

"Is he a relation?"

"No, not at all. He works about the place, and my aunt looks after him."

I noticed she was biting her lip. I was unsettling

her. It was a good feeling. She had been unsettling me for long enough. "That's a convenient arrangement."

"Yes."

"You sound doubtful."

"Well, to be honest, I don't like him being here."

"You're not as charitable as your aunt."

"Oh, it's not exactly charity. They're quite close. He's been living with my aunt for nine years now."

"What, you mean intimately?"

"Yes. Well, I suppose so."

"They didn't seem like a likely couple to me. That's great."

Niamh looked away. Then she walked up onto the beach and sat down on the sand. I followed her. "You don't seem enthusiastic."

"I don't like the situation. I feel Maurice is being used. She doesn't care for him, it just suits her to have him around. He stops her having to come to terms with loneliness, and he's undemanding. In a small place like this, you can imagine the talk. His family has disowned him, no other employer will touch him. He has no dignity left."

"I think you're just suffering from a legacy of convent education. Surely it's his decision where he sleeps."

She looked at me steadily. "Don't you understand? Maurice is simple. Mentally, just a small child."

She looked down and began to put on her shoes. I felt ridiculous. We were silent for some time. When I spoke again, it was quietly. "Her husband's dead, I suppose?"

Niamh laughed bitterly and pointed idiotically at the horizon. "He's out there somewhere! They had the bungalow built and moved here from Dublin. They never had any children of their own, and I think they began to bore each other after I left. They needed a challenge. He had a lot of experience in business, and he wanted to stop the drift to the city, contribute something to the West. His eyes shone when he talked about it, he looked like he was twenty years old. I don't know what happened to all the plans. Once the house was built he seemed to lose interest. Well, he upped and left and went to America. There was some talk about a local girl, but I don't know if there's any truth in it. He has his sister post money home to my aunt regularly, but never a word. She never knows where he is. After twenty-five years of married life! She never says anything, but it must be killing her. It must be killing him too, but I doubt he admits it." We sat looking out at the sky and the sea. The storm was passing and the great, black clouds were pulling apart. Far out, a fan of sun beamed through, like something out of a holy picture. There seemed very little left to say. The magnificence of it embarrassed me.

"There's something oppressive about this place," I said.

She considered carefully and then began to speak with quiet conviction. "I don't find that now. But you've got to be strong enough for it."

I was forced to remark inwardly on the originality of her character. But I couldn't agree with her. "Look at that wildness, the powerful sea, the sand. It breaks people. The land crumbles into it. Look at those rocks over there, clenched against the sea, and that house sagging into the ground." But her eyes were so strong

I had to lower my face.

"The reason that house is a ruin has got to be remembered, but hunger is just one interpretation for this landscape. It's all passion, surely you can see that? It doesn't break you, if you're passionate enough for it."

She stood and faced the sea, and then began to run in and out along the water's edge, keeping pace with the rush and retreat of the waves. I got up to run after her. I could see her legs gracefully stretching out one after the other as the sea lapped in and out on the sand. My legs were like lead, I couldn't seem to control them, but I persevered, and I saw she was gradually slowing down, she was letting me catch her up. When I reached her she caught my hand and pulled me, laughing, up to the house. We went into her room. It faced the sea and I saw a huge painting on an easel beside the window. Everything in the room was beautiful. She had managed to clear away the worst of Mrs Flanagan's fussy ornamentation, and there was a great woollen cover on her bed in soft pinks and greens and browns. I lay down on it, winded, and she made real coffee on a little gas stove. I sipped at it, and we didn't say anything when she started to work. I don't know whether I slept or just lay there, watching her turning and touching, listening to the waves rush in and rush out.

And so the painting began to take shape. Every afternoon I lay there, day after day. The weather was so changeable she had to paint inside. Her view was hampered, of course, but still she got the lines of it exactly, the peaks of the mountains and the sweeps between them, the clear curves of the sea coming in, and the tide marks on the strand. She said she sometimes felt it must be a system of hieroglyphics, perfectly comprehensible if only you gave up all hope of translating. I asked her once did she have no ambition to work from her imagination rather than from nature. She said that her painting was always the product of her imagination, her peculiar way of seeing. She said that her painting represented her effort to reach outside herself, rather than inside, but that the effort itself made the painting. I can still hear her voice as she said that. I hadn't known how intelligent women could be until I met Niamh. I suspected them all of my mother's obtuseness. I don't think you realise, perhaps, how beautiful she looked when she painted. Her concentration was total, her movements slow, but perfectly controlled. Every now and then, she would glance over to see if I was still looking. I became important to her, you see. She said to me once, laughing, that she could never paint without me again, without my interest and belief. This was the most beautiful painting she had ever done. I almost felt I had fathered it.

Sometimes she worked for her aunt in the morning, but sometimes she came walking with me. We explored the island, the nearby peninsula, staggering over hard tufts of luminous green grass, eyed with suspicion by the chewing sheep. She brought me to a ruined castle, a crumbling graveyard, a deserted beach, where she announced she was going swimming and began to take off her clothes. I turned quickly and walked towards the road and she laughed so hard she had to hold her middle. We had never touched, you see. The first time was when a

German car drew up and someone tried to photograph us walking along a bog. She grabbed me then, and swung me to the ground, and we lay there, hidden and giggling until the car drove on.

The only pub was miles away, and so we spent the long, dark evenings in Niamh's room. Sometimes she took a bottle of whiskey from under her bed and we drank it in our coffee. She told me all about herself, she would talk for hours. Her mother had died soon after she was born, and her father had left to find work in England. She couldn't communicate with him now, he was like a stranger. He had a "floozy," as she put it and Niamh couldn't stand the sight of her. She had lived with her aunt and uncle until she was eighteen, and then she went to art school in Wales, doing odd jobs to get by. She'd lived in Dublin since then, most of the time with some man she was going to marry, but didn't in the end. Her mouth twisted up when she talked about that. She came down here more and more now, her friends talked of nothing but nappies and mortgages. She was happier alone, she said. I didn't believe that. Sometimes she would take my hand and look into my eyes so that I failed to concentrate on what I was saying. But I always took my hand away. I knew she wanted me and it was that that repelled me. I was twenty-two years old and far from totally inexperienced, but no young woman had ever taken my hand before. Sometimes she would gaze at my body when I stood up to go, and the open look in her eyes frightened me.

I talked to her though. I can't forget that. It was as if part of me passed into her keeping. I wasn't frightened when I was talking to her, she lulled me with her silent face, her quick smile. But when I shut my door at night the darkness closed in on me. I hated myself for losing my pride, my identity, for upholding the bourgeois illusion that something can work out for the best, that a life can be changed. I tossed then, the panic closing in on me. I swear I hated her then. My sick imagination had her gossiping with my mother at the tea-table about how I could be brought round if only you had the knack. My mother, smiling, thinking there's nothing can go wrong with a young man a good woman can't cure. Then sometimes the noise of Maurice's whinging cry reached me and I covered my face with my pillow and squeezed my eyes tight. But the fresh air, the walking, the whiskey, defeated the panic and I always fell asleep before long. And in the morning a glimmer of sun would waken the colours of the scenery as I ate my breakfast in the dining-room. And Niamh's bright face and strong eyes dispersed my fears of deception.

I can't find expression. I can find words of course—I have mentioned my erudition. It's that the words I find push me on towards a flamboyance that has nothing to do with me, grey wall, grey house, grey road. But I must write it. Maybe if I wrote it I could understand and so, forget. I have become so unsure of myself.

That last night was different in lots of ways. Niamh got drunk, she began to tell me about her ex-lover. She would tug at my sleeve when she told me to give her something. I had nothing to give. I as good as told her so. I think she was starting to cry when I left. I shut my door, but I couldn't sleep. I couldn't let her think there was cause for hope, any hope. There is no more dangerous thing than hope, except love, of course, but they're the same thing, I suppose. I couldn't sleep, I saw her wet eyes as I turned away, Christ. Then about two in the morning I heard Maurice's wails of fear. You can't imagine a better expression for the emotion of human terror. I heard Mrs Flanagan's footsteps, her muffled words of comfort and entreaty. But Maurice would not be silenced so easily that night. It was as if the world stayed still to listen to that terrible sound. I put my pillow over my head, but even if the noise was deadened, I carried it still in my mind. Suddenly I felt a hand on my shoulder, and I battled, terrified, from beneath the pillow. It was only Niamh, Niamh standing there in her nightdress. I saw desperation in her face, and she clutched my shoulder, whispering, "Let's get away from this." I nodded my assent, and she went back to her room to put on her clothes.

We met in the hall and stole out the back door. We went, instinctively, towards the beach. It was bitterly cold. Niamh was shivering, and she thrust her hand through my unwilling arm. Her arm, her hand, they were the only warm, recognisable human things I could feel. We didn't speak at all, we just walked slowly along the sand beside the black, lapping water. I think we were both privately terrified by that thick darkness. Suddenly rain began to beat against our faces—it one of those squalls that drift in so frequently off the Atlantic. We turned and began to run back, filled with irrational fear. The rain poured down, our clothes were sticking to us. We seemed to have been running for ages, when we hit grass again. We had missed the path to the house and were climbing the hill towards the disused cottage. Niamh knew the ground well, and holding my arm tightly, she moved to the left, stretching her hand out to feel a wall. She stopped and then moved carefully sideways again until she felt the door, which pushed open quite easily. We stumbled gladly in, laughing with relief. I took a few steps forward, and hit an old tractor, and Niamh laughed again and, holding my arm, brought me towards a stack of musty hay in the corner. She sat down and guided me down too. Then she struggled out of her coat and began to unbutton mine, but I broke roughly away from her hands.

"You're soaking... I just thought I'd help you get off your wet coat..."

I realised my mistake. She hesitated a moment, but yes, this time she was going to say it, "Why are you so frightened?"

"I'm not frightened."

"Why are you so unhappy, then?"

"That's what the psychiatrist called me, 'unhappy.' You're as bad as him."

"Maybe he was right."

She was upsetting me, I cast desperately round for words, but something blocked me, I couldn't find any. When I spat out "I hate doctors" her response was inevitable.

"Why make that sort of statement, Dermot? You can't generalise like that."

"I trust none of them. They're liars."

"When has a doctor ever lied to you?"

I could hear her exasperation. I don't know why I felt the need to vindicate myself. I told her about my father. He was a quiet, gentle man with a soft Mayo accent, not like my mother, bawling this moment from the kitchen—"Dermot, yer tea's ready, love." He was very cultured, read widely in both Irish and English literature, but that didn't get him a livelihood in country Mayo. There was no money to send him to teacher training college, and so he came to Dublin with the aim of saving it. The only job he could find was in a factory. Then there was my mother to support, and soon I came along, but he didn't complain, he worked long and he worked hard. One day when I was eight years old he came home early, and he looked so different I was afraid to go near him. From then on, I only saw him in hospital, and he had the smell of disinfectant off him. He was never really my father again. It was no surprise when they said he was dead, I had been expecting it, I was numbed. My mother grasped my hand so tightly at the funeral, I screamed and wrenched it away. She has never held it since. I kept my pain to myself, I made myself hard. It wasn't until a year later that I read an article on asbestos dust in the doctor's waiting-room. All my vague suspicions gelled together then. I understood. When I saw the doctor I asked him about my father, but he said nonsense, a bad heart is a bad heart. I saw no reason to believe him, I had been fooled so mightily and so completely up to now. I nodded docilely, but inside I was closing up. And so I learned to nod docilely in every situation, and to tot up the reality, privately, all the while. I made every attempt not to be fooled again.

What you don't perhaps understand is that I had never told that to anyone before. I felt weak, as if something had gone from me. She was silent, she was taking on my pain. She put her arm round me and I lay against her shoulder. I think I may have been crying. She tightened her arms around me and held me like a child. Then it was as if a shudder went through her. No—I try to write this every day and every day I fail. It was as if something took her over. I tried to hold back but she wouldn't let me. There was command in her body. She held me steady and began to kiss my hair, refusing to countenance denial. I shut my eyes and tried not to feel it, and then she began to speak, to whisper, give, give.

"What do you want?" I said.

"Trust me, trust somebody once in your life."

I couldn't find it in myself to ask her again what she wanted. I just loosened my body against her, and the knot of pain, the item by which I recognised myself, dissolved away. I can't find the words to write exactly what happened then. I know that the rain stopped and the sky cleared and the moon shone in the window, casting a criss-cross of light on the ground. I remember lying on my back looking at the ceiling, the walls, the grey stones clutching each other with varying success. She lay against me and I remember I couldn't stop touching her, the soft tangle of her hair, each curve and hollow. It was as if I was mapping something out, and yet the map would never be made. There was no translation for that degree of pleasure.

It was almost light when we got back to the house. We kissed in the corridor, I remember, and went back to our rooms, shutting the door behind us. I got into bed and closed my eyes, and I was warm and happy. I was thinking of Niamh, and the arms around me were her arms. I nearly fell asleep, but before I could slip into oblivion, I began to ask, suddenly, about myself. It was like another voice in my head saying, yes, but what about you, what are you now? I grew more wakeful, even anxious. The arms around me became my own again. They tried to ascertain the shape of my identity, but they couldn't find any. It was like waking out of a dream. I sat bolt upright and found my image in the dressing-table mirror. I felt estranged from it. This is so hard to write. I know it was derangement, I am sane enough to know that. And yet I believe in the truth of my feelings then. Perhaps I articulated them in an awkward manner, but they were true, nevertheless. There was no future, no hope, for myself and Niamh. In my panic I blamed her for duping me into playing along, but we were both dupes—that is clear to me now. It was not my fault that I confused the issue at the time.

She doesn't know I realise my mistake. It is all over now, anyway. It all happened a long time ago. I remember how the rage grew, taking me over. I imagined Niamh sitting in bed, a smile of triumph on her face. I had to have the last word. I had to assert myself again. Then I would leave—there was a bus from the nearest town at ten. I got out of bed and threw on my clothes, I crept down the corridor. But when I opened the door the sight of her sleeping form disarmed me. I had pictured her sitting up, waiting to greet me with a confident smile. I moved towards the bed, but it seemed so violent to wake her. My hesitation frustrated me, I quivered with suppressed anger. I swear I don't know what came over me then. There is no valid explanation, that is what I must face. I took my penknife out of my anorak pocket, threw off the sheet, and spliced the painting diagonally, once, twice, again, again. I looked round, but she was sleeping peacefully. I think I had expected her to scream. I felt no satisfaction, and I threw the sheet back over my handiwork, I don't know why. She sighed and I was sure she would waken, so I walked quickly towards the door. I turned to look at her again, but she tossed in her sleep, and I hurried out.

I began to throw my things into my case when I got back to my room, but after a few minutes I heard Niamh's door open. I froze. I heard her pass my room and go out into the yard to take her aunt's bike. The wheels rattled over the cow-ramp. I finished my packing and left Mrs Flanagan's money on the hall-table. I gave Niamh a chance to get far enough away, then I let myself out into the fresh morning, out into the road. I began to walk briskly, but soon I heard a low noise and turned to see a car snaking towards me from a distance. I stuck out my thumb when it rounded the corner, and it drew up. I knew the face of the driver, a farmer living nearby. He and his son were going into town. The older man grunted amicably from time to time, while the younger swivelled in his seat to talk me. "Were you on your holidays, you were? Up from Dublin, is it? Ah, it's nice scenery, but sure we don't get the weather." The car slowed suddenly, the farmers waved. I saw it was Niamh and sank behind my case. The car crept past and she held her bike up on the verge, smiling, waving. I saw her face. I saw her basket full of Christ knows, Christ knows, honey, fresh milk, the more expensive tea. The car gripped the surface as best it could, and gathered its strength for a hill.

Planting

It is very quiet now. But there's something in the air. A smell, maybe. A smell of burning. I am an old man now. My son has left me lying here in my bed. He has heard there is trouble in the city, and has gone to see. There will always be trouble. It is natural that there be trouble. Stupidity and short-sightedness, all of it. Not on the part of the kings and councillors. They were clever. But we were the pawns. It all starts to go wrong if men act like pawns.

She had green eyes and red hair. I had never seen a woman so beautiful. I wanted her. I would have done anything to have her. I was the third son. I was farming a piece of land given me out of charity and little bigger than a handkerchief. The harvests came worse and worse. There were too many people, there was no work. I imagined her body under her yellow dress and I was desperate. She wanted me all right, in her way. But she knew I had nothing. It was 1610 and the notices started coming out. Land in Ulster. At first I ignored them. But then I began to think about it. What were my prospects if I stayed? I needed her. And so I asked her to come with me. I told her how low the rent would be on the land, and how easy it would be to get rich. A beautiful, fertile wilderness was just waiting, I said, for the hand of the cultivator. There was a whimsical adventurousness in her. And she surprised me by saying yes.

That was when the hard part started. I had been happy in Ayrshire. I was close to my family. I liked my little cottage. But the image of her body was always before me and there was nothing I could do. I sold the land back to my brother and I bought a ticket. Moira and I were married. I brought her back to the little cottage, where we lived a few days of frenzied ecstasy. But soon my brother wanted the house back and we packed up our belongings. I said goodbye to the family, my mother weeping, my father silent, sad. I knew there was no good in the old dog and that he'd die of starvation or go for the sheep. So I called him and held his head between my knees and put a bullet through it.

The wind in my face and the boat heaving, Moira sick against me. It was night-time when we struggled ashore, and looked at the blackness around us. If I had known then that I would never leave that shore...But all I cared about was getting to shelter. The cart rattled through the night—full of shadows and eyes, but nothing attacked. We reached a small, stone house, lit candles and lay down as we were on our sacks of grain. I don't know if Moira slept, but I stayed awake listening to the mice dance in the loft and rallying my courage to face the light.

I went out early. That first glimpse of my land...My land. It was late autumn and the fields were charred, for the Irish burn the straw after harvest and move on. But even so I could see the potential of it. Great heavy trees. I reached and scooped up a handful of black soil and smelt it. I knew I would have no difficulty growing fat on land like that. I looked back towards the house and I saw Moira, a shape in white beside the house. She was looking out too. I ran back to her, skipping and yelling, and as I approached, I saw the excitement in her face. But there was a sort of distance in her too, even then. She didn't look at me straight. And she seemed absent-minded when I talked to her.

The plantation had a tight, active social life, centred around the church. We were desperate to preserve an air of normality and civilisation. There were very few of us and we knew it. We made as much noise as we could. And every so often Abercorn threw open his private land and set long, wooden tables out on the lawns. We talked only of the future and always with optimism. We didn't talk about our fears. If we had they would have risen up and gripped us by the throat. Everyone noticed Moira, of course, and she loved it. I remember watching her glow and shine beside me at Christmas, as the stares came quicker, thicker. I held her hand under the table. She talked to me but I knew she wasn't paying me any attention. She loved the admiration. I had a sick feeling inside. I brought her home that evening and I made her lie down under me. I wanted to claim her utterly for myself. But of course, it was impossible. She could lie under me as long as she liked, I couldn't know what was in her mind. There began to be new ribbons on her bonnet, discreet but beautiful. She stalked out to church like a black cat with its tail in the air. She knew what those severe clothes did for her. The eyes swung to her when she walked in the door.

If I had thought about anything clearly then, I

would have known what would happen. To Moira and me. To the plantation. We didn't really think of the Irish as owning anything, because they had a different idea of the land from us. They thought of it as a shifting thing that existed only as long as the crops grew, whereas for us it was steady, our stake in reality, the land our children would marry on. They began to be put off, sent to less fertile parts, or made to pay vast rents for the land they had always farmed. Grey-faced families walking for miles, going for miles on crude carts. But all I could think about was Moira, where she was, what she was thinking. I began to find excuses to keep her at home. I wanted to plant a child in her to claim her, to bind her to me. She let me have my way, laughing quietly. But I couldn't smash the glass of those eyes and get inside.

There is a smell, a smell of burning. It is stronger now. If I had the strength I'd get up and see what it was. But no, no, I won't. If it were in the house I'd hear it. It's outside. And yes...there are shouts. People calling for help. I am too old to be of any use. I lie here and go over the past, over and over. Though it all happened thirty years ago or more, and everything has changed. There is a papist king, trouble in England, trouble everywhere.

That spring I sowed my land for the first time. The pleasure that was, watching the seed pass into the rich earth. I was out all day at it, but I told Moira to keep to the house. We neighbours shared the work amongst us, every able man did his bit. I was happier than I had been in months. I came home at night exhausted and sat with Moira an hour or so before I fell asleep. I should have known that there was something queer because she was so quiet and amiable. That smile of hers. I should have known. Almost every able man was working, but there was one missing. It was a hot afternoon and for some reason I felt sick to my stomach. I watched the seed fall to the ground and that terrible fatigue came on me, the grey fatigue you get looking at what you have most desired. Overwork, I thought, and I made my way back to the house. And yes, I heard them when I entered, but all my strength left me and I didn't go in. I stood in the kitchen until I heard her name him, and then I turned and walked into the fields. I said nothing all through that terrible summer while the Irish were put off the land, I said nothing as the grain swelled. I said nothing either as Moira swelled. I had often wished her dead rather than have another man look at her. And I blamed myself when she died in childbirth that winter.

Everything has changed. And yet nothing. I never married again. Moira's face is before me always. I know I didn't love her as a man should love his wife. She didn't deserve it, anyway. But it would have been difficult to settle for the gentle generosity of love after passion like that. Her son, Samuel...He has nothing of her, but a lot of her family. I sometimes wonder is he mine. I have spent whole evenings trying to trace my face in his. But now I don't care. What matter as long as he is strong and industrious. I cared for nothing after Moira's death, and I worked very little. It wasn't easy to nurse the land back to fertility, but he did it. He is not a friendly boy, but there was little friendliness shown him. If he came back now he would know what to do. Instead I lie here and do nothing. I do nothing about the glare on the wall, the thick smell of smoke. I feel I have nothing to defend. Let them! I have no part in this plantation. I lost my wits in the ruthless pursuit of a single greed, and when I was cheated of that there was nothing left. Love could have tempered it, I could have shared, bent, compromised. I did none of those things. When I shut my eyes I see before me the body of the woman I bartered my brains for. And I am happy to shut my eyes and lie still.

Raving Autumn

The Atlantic pushes in on the land in great silver fingers on the south-west coast of Ireland. It has done so for centuries and centuries of passers-by must have marvelled at this interplay of sea and land. It is relatively recently that people came with the will and the money to mark the landscape with complementary beauty, and so claim it for themselves. Moyle House was built in the Georgian style and its great windows faced south. More recently still the Duckworth family bought the house, and now we see Major Duckworth and his wife Lucinda, in their drawing-room, looking out. They are moving their heads in time to the music which comes from the piano in the corner. Elizabeth, their only child, sits in a blue velvet dress with a blue velvet bow in her long, fair hair, moving her fingers carefully up and down the keys as she has been taught, sending great draughts of Mozart out to the garden and the bay and the Atlantic.

But the power of these people did not last, and Moyle House is no longer there. Nothing remains except that the ground is bricky and uneven. The Duckworths are long since dead, and the sea listens only to itself.

Let us imagine the girl at the piano had a maid—as indeed, she must have had. Let us give her a head of red hair like something off the cover of a cheap paperback. Mary's mother too had worked for the Duckworths. But Mary was not happy with her lot. It was 1919, and times were changing. She was pretty and intelligent and she felt she was made for better things than fetching and carrying for a spoilt fifteen-year old. Major Duckworth was scarcely ever there, his wife was distant and dim. And Mary made use of the disorganisation of the household to slip out and join Cumann na mBan, which had recently started up in the village. She believed in the movement as much because she had wanted to be a teacher and it hadn't been possible, and because she was sick and tired of being looked down on, as because she wanted an independent Ireland in the abstract. She met a group of young people, united in a cause and naturally, she fell in love. She fell in love with Thomas, a volunteer, and not much more than twenty. Let us give him dark hair and dark eyes.

Mary had a romantic nature. She took an immediate dislike to Liam Cullen, the man co-ordinating military activity in the area. He was tall and stout with a pink complexion and thinning, sandy hair, and his eyes were strong, blue and steely. He was respected for his discipline and nerve. He had fought in the Great War and was convinced that the IRA had no chance if its discipline was not as tight as that of the British army. Mary agreed with this in theory. Perhaps it was Liam's lack of personal grace that irritated her. Once, angered by the shooting of a frightened young IRA man who informed under torture, Mary told Thomas she thought Cullen was taking vengeance on creation for his own ugliness. But Thomas looked so shocked, she took it back. Then Cullen found out that Major Duckworth himself was co-ordinating a ring of British Army informers in the area, and he planned to raid Moyle and try the Major for treason against the Irish Republic. And Mary furnished plans of Moyle to the volunteers, because now the balance of power between herself and her employer had changed. She knew the raid would mean the end of her double life as maid and re-volutionary, it would mean freedom.

But there was a contrasting current in Mary's mind, and this is the nub of the story. Her heart was heavy for the old house. She had been brought up to clean and polish the wrought-iron banister, to rub the silver service so it came up well. She had been brought up to brush Elizabeth's hair until it shone like silk and to tie blue velvet ribbons in her hair. She and Elizabeth were like sisters, like mother and daughter. Elizabeth's siblings faded out and died. Throughout her echoing childhood, Mary was the one intimate. Mary knew Elizabeth better than anyone, she felt close to her without actually liking her. It would have been very difficult to like anyone as spoilt as Elizabeth, with her snarling "Stop tearing my hair, you're hurting me!" But Mary was fascinated by her high pale beauty. She couldn't help admiring her, and in weak moments, even envying her. Mostly people print themselves on the minds of others in a moment, and Elizabeth's moment in Mary's was this. She was sitting at a piano with the lamplight on her yellow hair and blue velvet skirt, her long pale fingers running up and down the keys. The music was beautiful, sweet and haunting, and Mary stood in the hall a moment and listened. That was all.

The leaves were red and yellow and gold on the ancient trees around the old house. The plan matured. It was decided that on the night of the raid Mary should slip out and wait for Thomas in an outhouse at the boundary of the estate, rather than openly identify herself with the volunteers. That night she sat brushing Elizabeth's hair and looking out into the wet night. She went on brushing mechanically for much longer than necessary, until Elizabeth's eyes closed and her head sagged. Mary put her to bed and sat for a moment in the rose-lit room, her hand on the white lace quilt. There would be no more of this, there would be no more elegance. She would be Thomas's woman. The reality of it struck her for the first time and she began to panic. Everything would be different. She looked out at the dark night from a window which would no longer be there in the morning. She would have no window. Elizabeth would be fleeing to England with her mother, and they would never see each other again. No, it was impossible, it was too much of a loss. It would mean losing her past, her values, the whole foundation of her sensibility. She did something very strange because she was panicking, and half an hour later she was sitting at the window of the summerhouse smoothing Elizabeth's hair, trying to comfort her. And presently they saw the great glow of the fire, and Mary pushed Elizabeth's face against her, and then they heard shouts, and so she covered Elizabeth's ears. And she was glad she had, because then she heard the two shots that killed the Major.

That night Liam screamed at Mary, "Are you out of your mind, woman? We can't keep her with us."

And Mary said, "She's only fifteen, she can change. We can't leave her to that kind of life. I'm not leaving her to some English maid and that bitch of a mother. She can change and then she'll be happier."

Only later did Mary admit to herself that she had been talking nonsense. She had taken Elizabeth with her because she was beautiful.

The next morning they were sitting round the table, Thomas, Mary, Seán, Neil and his wife Cáit. The bedroom door opened and Elizabeth was standing there. Nobody spoke. The girl took in the faces one by one. Mary said, "Are you hungry, Elizabeth?" and Elizabeth nodded. She sat back by the wall and Mary cut bread for her, handed her a plate. But then Elizabeth's head dropped, the plate hit against the stone. And Mary felt what madness it had been to take her away. She followed Elizabeth into the bedroom and shut the door. The girl was sobbing and she turned on Mary. "Who are those people?"

"They're my friends."

"Why did you take me here?"

"To keep you safe."

"Safe from what?"

"From the raiders that were in the house."

"Why can't I go to my parents?"

"They've gone back to England. And it wouldn't be safe for you to travel just yet."

Elizabeth threw herself onto the bed and sobbed, and Mary was sick with guilt. She sat beside Elizabeth and tried to comfort her, but the girl's sobbing grew louder and harder, and finally Mary left. When she opened the door the men around the table peered in, and when she closed it they began to laugh, but the look on Mary's face shut them up.

Those were difficult times. The country was being combed for Liam's column. Cáit and Neil's house was a well-kept secret, but no-one knew how long it would last. It was understood that Mary and Thomas were to get married as soon as the war was over, and Mary already acted the part of a wife. Thomas was round the house a lot, lying low after Moyle, and Mary loved to be with him. She loved to see his socks tangled up with her stockings on the chair, to use the same towel as he did. But still she tasted imperfectly the first days of her freedom. Elizabeth was a silence between them, and it was worse when the silence broke.

"Have you been thinking what we should do with Elizabeth?"

"Do with her?"

"You know she can't go back."

"Yes."

"So?"

"She never loved her parents anyway. I was the closest person to her. We can bring her round to our way of seeing things."

"Her whole background is different to ours."

"She's only a child. She trusts us. She'll learn to understand."

But far from understanding, Elizabeth maintained an icy silence. She sat on the bed and looked out the window. Her behaviour made a mockery of Mary's words.

On the sixth day, when Mary was dressing the girl's hair as usual, she said, "Who's in Moyle House now, if my parents have left?"

Mary hesitated. "No-one," she said.

Elizabeth began again. "That fire was coming from Moyle that night, wasn't it?"

"Yes."

"Is there anything left of it, or did it burn to the ground?"

Mary found it hard to speak. "It burned to the ground," she said.

She expected Elizabeth to go silent or hit out. Instead she turned and looked straight at her.

"Did the Shinners do it? The same as they did to the Montagues?"

"I think so."

"They're wicked, evil people."

Mary was stung. "Do you know how many houses the British army have burned down, Elizabeth?"

The girl said nothing for a moment. Then she said, "Yes, but it's not the same thing."

"It's worse for a poor person if their house is burned down. The IRA protect those people. All of us here are in it."

Elizabeth's mouth dropped open. "How could you be so evil?"

"Isn't it evil to take away a country's freedom?" Elizabeth started to scream and Mary lunged towards her to stop the noise. The girl turned from her viciously and was quiet.

But the next day Mary heard whispering in the bedroom in the early morning as she set the fire. She opened the door and saw Elizabeth hanging out the window, whispering hoarsely at the air. When she heard Mary she jumped back. Mary pushed her aside and looked into the astonished face of the young postman. Of course he had known it was an IRA house. He was prepared to turn a blind eye, but not to get involved. But Mary knew the sight of Elizabeth Duckworth would be likely to turn his head with promises of glamour and importance and hopes of reward. She knew she should go straight to Liam. But he would want to silence either the postman or the girl. And she feared he would choose the girl. She felt she might save the situation if she acted fast.

She said, "Wait there or by God you'll be sorry." And he was waiting for her when she got out. By now he was looking self-important.

"I can trust you to stay loyal to your own country and not to another," said Mary, sounding him out.

The young postman stuck out his chin. "You might," he said.

Mary felt panic grip her, but she controlled it. She slapped his soft, fat cheek soundly and said, "You will or you won't be long for this world."

The young postman closed and opened his eyes. "Do you hear?" insisted Mary.

"I do," said the young postman.

"The last man who informed found himself dead on top of a barbed wire fence with the word 'informer' tied around his neck."

The young postman's eyes bulged. "I swear," he said.

"I'm warning you," said Mary and she turned. The young postman grabbed his bike and was half-way down the path before he hit the saddle.

Mary went into the bedroom. She felt sick with herself, she had a dark throbbing in her head. Things were going badly. Elizabeth was sitting on the bed, half-crying. "What's going to happen to the young postman?" she said.

"I don't know," Mary said cruelly and sat down. "I don't know what's going to happen to us."

"I'm sorry," Elizabeth almost whispered.

"It's not enough to be sorry. We could all be shot dead because of your selfishness."

"I didn't understand."

"You understood well enough." Mary stood at the window lost in the dark throbbing of her head. It was some minutes later that Elizabeth's crying broke through. Mary felt sorry for her suddenly— it wasn't her fault, God knows. She put her arms round her and said, "Sssh!"

Elizabeth couldn't stop for a long time and then she sat gulping for air like a fish. And she said, "My room and my books and my piano. I don't know where my dogs are."

And Mary thought of the flames eating up the precious volumes, eating the gleaming piano, sending the King Charles spaniels mad with terror into the dark trees. She said nothing of these thoughts, but Elizabeth must have felt her sympathy, because from then on she accepted all the affection she was offered.

It was about this time that the Black and Tans shot Seán's father in front of his wife and young son and burnt out their house. They stayed in Cáit and Neil's for two days, a weeping woman and a puzzled child. Some one had informed and a campaign against informers began. Night after night they went out in the uniforms of dead auxiliaries, and spying peasants and landed loyalists were deceived and indicted. They were shot dead. The raiders lived the life of party-addicts, sleeping by day, going out by night, drinking to keep up their courage. Mary hardly knew Thomas as he was now. He had made himself so strong it was difficult to communicate with him. He was embarrassed about Mary's attentions to Elizabeth because he knew they exasperated Liam. Once he found out she'd given Elizabeth the only bit of meat in the house, and he was furious.

"We can't keep her here much longer, Mary, they'll trace her here. And once they get her, she'll tell them everything. We can't let her out of our sight. I don't know what our alternatives are." And Mary got frightened for the girl. She promised Thomas that she would bring Elizabeth into the movement, but she didn't even know how to begin.

By now the men had lost their shyness of Elizabeth and they teased and baited her if they thought Mary was out of earshot. It shocked Mary that Elizabeth should be treated in this way. She had always seen the girl's beauty as something cold and remote, like a chandelier or a page of music. But now she saw that men admired her without reverence, as a woman among others. She had always seen Elizabeth as a child, because that was how she had been treated at Moyle. But now she was sixteen. One night Mary was drinking with Thomas and a crowd of people in the kitchen when she heard voices in the bedroom. She tried to loosen herself from Thomas's grasp, but he was drinking, he held her. Finally she got loose. Seán was in there with Elizabeth. He was a good lad, he hadn't wanted to frighten her, but he was rough and spoke strangely, and Elizabeth had never been touched by a man before. She sat on the end of the bed, crying and shivering.

There was a terrible scene. Mary acted as if Elizabeth had been raped, as if her only daughter had been raped. Liam defended Seán like a son accused of rape, and they faced each other, enemies. In truth, Mary was unhappy with the campaign, the drinking, the roughness, the deaths. Liam resented this in her, resented her protective attitude towards Elizabeth, symbol of a society he hated. But the difference was argued out in the specific terms of the night's events.

"So he tried to kiss the girl. Isn't she sixteen and isn't it time she was kissed."

"She's still a child. She doesn't know anything."

"I wouldn't be so sure about that, the way she keeps herself so nice. My God, she's honoured he looked at her, coming from where she does."

"He knew she wasn't used to anything like that. He terrified her."

"It's about time she got in touch with reality. That bedroom's like the last outpost of the British empire. I won't have you heating her water or doing her hair any more."

"Are you going to order me round now? What can you do about it?"

"You know I can do plenty about it. What any sane man would do."

Mary stormed into the bedroom and closed the door. She comforted the girl. She had been brought up to brush Elizabeth's hair until it shone like silk, and to tie blue velvet ribbons in her hair. She brushed, not knowing whether she did it to soothe Elizabeth or herself. But towards morning Thomas came to her and gently he put it to her that she should take Elizabeth away for the girl's own sake as well as the men's. Five miles away on the coast was a tiny house, left empty by a dead volunteer. The lights would not thus be suspicious, and Mary and Elizabeth could hide out. And there was another reason for Mary to get into safety. She suspected she was pregnant.

It was hard for her to say goodbye to Thomas. Every day he was at risk, and it was hard to be cut off from him. But she made Liam promise to send news immediately if anything happened. Elizabeth was still very quiet, she kept her face averted from Seán all the time. Mary couldn't find it in herself to talk to him either. But when the men left, things became much simpler, and a peace came over the two young women. The cottage was completely isolated, on a beach backed by sheer cliffs. Mary could see Elizabeth relax. She looked happier than she had been since Moyle—happier than she had ever been, maybe. It was almost as it was in Moyle; they had their own small universe. They went running along the beach, the roar in their ears, the sun sparkling on the sea. They could hardly speak against the wind. Elizabeth's cheeks were red and there was a brightness in her eyes that Mary had never seen before.

A few mornings later Mary came into the bedroom with a basin of hot water. Elizabeth was sitting up in bed, waiting. Then she said, "It seems a bit strange, somehow."

Mary was mixing the hot water with the cold. She looked up and said, "What does?"

Elizabeth smiled nervously. "It seems a bit strange that you get up and heat the water for me and I never heat it for you. It seems a bit strange."

Mary didn't know what to say. "I do it from habit," she said. "It's no trouble to me anyway, I'm used to it."

"Maybe I should learn some of those things. I'll need to know them. You won't always be living with me."

"You'll have another maid."

"Not if things change the way Thomas said they would."

Mary's voice rose higher. "But you'd never want to be cooking and cleaning and God knows what for a husband and a rake of children."

Mary looked at Elizabeth, and it was strange, she was smiling brightly. She had that glow on her face that Mary had seen the first day at the cottage. It is disturbing to think you know everything about a person, and then to realise that some of her thoughts have been utterly hidden from you. It takes away the veneer of certainty given with such difficulty to the world. Mary began to panic, she repeated herself, "You won't want to be doing any of that. Even if we get independence, you'll be back to England as soon as the troubles end."

Elizabeth's face was serious. She looked very adult, suddenly. She said, "I feel free in this house. I was very lonely at Moyle, I never saw anyone. I hardly saw my father and I hate my mother. I'd love if I could find a way of being free." She sat on the bed and Mary lifted the silver-backed brush because she had been brought up to brush Elizabeth's hair until it shone like silk, and to tie blue velvet ribbons in her hair. And then Elizabeth said, smiling. "Let me brush my own hair this morning," which in a small way, was the beginning of the end.

Elizabeth began to do her share of the few basic tasks there were about the house, and Mary kept on saying to herself, it should be like this. They laughed together over Elizabeth's mistakes, they enjoyed each other's company. There was a new equality about their relationship. Elizabeth had been in a superior position before, but in a way, she had been completely in Mary's power. New lines had to drawn out for the relationship and it made for a lot of puzzlement and a lot of laughter. Elizabeth laughed more now, her face had grown wider, more womanly. It was not difficult to imagine her living in Ireland, the wife of some Irishman.

But Mary felt a strange cold feeling growing in her and as the days went by, she named it. It was anger. Perhaps it was to shock Elizabeth back to her old ways that she said one morning, "There's something I need to tell you about the raid, Elizabeth." Elizabeth looked up and Mary went on, "It's about your father. He was found guilty of informing on the IRA."

Mary was breathless, shocked at the words. But then Elizabeth said, "Was he shot?" and Mary said, "Yes."

Elizabeth paled and sat down suddenly. After a moment she said, "What kind of informing?"

"He organised a spy ring and collected detailed information. Some of our people died because of it."

"You should have told me," Elizabeth said, but her

voice was steady.

"It would have upset you too much."

And Elizabeth said, "Yes, it might have done."

Mary felt embarrassed, she was almost apologetic, "He was passing information you see, he had to go. People were dying. He didn't care about them."

And Elizabeth said, "Yes, I can see that." Then she said, "It's surprising how far away from him I feel. Moyle seems a million years ago. It's as if it never existed, isn't it? It feels like you're talking about some one's father in a history book." She didn't cry, she was calm. Of course, Mary knew there had never been any love between the girl and her father, but she had thought respect, nostalgia...Elizabeth was letting it all run through her fingers, Moyle and everything it stood for. She was the one person who could have kept it alive for Mary, and now she was turning out just like everyone else. It was very cold now, the leaves were falling. Mary thought of the trees at Moyle, bare black fingers clenched in a circle, sheltering nothing. And she was so angry with Elizabeth that she couldn't speak. But she didn't let it show because she couldn't have explained it, even to herself.

The anger tightened in her. Several nights later she was lying in bed when she heard voices and wild knocking at the door. Elizabeth stirred but Mary said "Quiet!" They would have come for her and it was up with all of them. The knocking continued and the two girls lay still. The voices grew stronger and then there was a thud and then another one. They were forcing the door. There was nothing the women could do but lie there, their hearts knocking off their ribs. The thudding went on and then the voices came clear into the room. Mary stood up and threw a coat over her and opened the bedroom door and she felt arms around her and the smell of whiskey. She felt Thomas. When she looked round her again she saw them, Liam crazed-drunk and walking in circles, bottle in hand. Seán was looking fixedly across the room. He was looking at Elizabeth who was standing at the bedroom door, a vision in white. In a few minutes she re-emerged dressed, and she was smiling.

They were looking for her, alright. "Some one shopped us to that eejity postman," Thomas said. "They got it all out of him eventually, of course. They were coming for us and we were tipped off, and it's just as well. We had to turn tail and run out here, and who knows how long this place will hold?"

Liam was drunk; he sat on the table saying, "British cunt, we should get rid of her. Who knows how many good men her father did for and now she looks set to do for a few more. What do we owe her? We should shoot her like an old sheep-worrier." But Elizabeth didn't hear, she was talking to Seán. And Mary had the blood humming in her ears because she was with Thomas and she couldn't focus too clearly on any-thing.

She took great gulps from the whiskey bottle and sat on Thomas's knee, and then they went into the bedroom and closed the door. It was wonderful to be with him again. They laughed and made love and all the time Mary could hear noise mingling with the throbbing in her head, and Liam's screams mingling with her own. Now Thomas was sleeping, not just love-tired, but exhausted from a series of sleepless nights. The whiskey was wearing off and Mary was cold. She tried to pull some of the covers off Thomas, but he was heavy and he was snoring now. Mary felt her irritation return. Where was this stupid-faced man now, was he even thinking about her? "Thomas?" She tried to pull at the cover. "Thomas?" He slept on. Her pleasure seemed pathetic to her suddenly. Transitory. Even if they survived and got married and raised the brat she was carrying, what would it mean? She'd still be cold and alone at night like this with a snoring stranger in the bed, only she'd be older and more worn out.

She could hear the noises in the kitchen clearly now, Liam swearing and thumping on the table. Suddenly she could have killed herself for leaving Elizabeth alone. She'd been drinking, she'd been crazy for Thomas, she hadn't thought. She felt sick with fear and she got up and struggled into her clothes.

Liam was singing now, beating time with his fists, "God save Ireland, say the heroes!

God save Ireland, say we all!"

Mary opened the door and Liam looked at her, those hard, steely eyes she hated. Elizabeth wasn't there. Mary shouted at Liam, "Where's the girl?"

He started to sing again, "Whether in the battlefield..." and Mary shouted, "Where's the girl?" and Liam sang louder. She went up to him and slapped his face, but Liam only looked surprised for a moment, and went on singing. Mary was sick with fear. She ran into the other room and out the front door, but there was no-one there and the night was silent. She went out the back and there was no-one there, then she heard voices and went closer. There were two figures sitting on the rough grass where the sand began. They weren't saying anything, and Mary knew to approach quietly. She saw the gleam of Elizabeth's hair cut in two by the black band of a boy's arm. Elizabeth was sitting in the dirt in the night kissing Seán O'Dowd.

Mary didn't say anything, but that night she dreamt about the fire. There was a roaring and a crackling and Liam and Thomas were outside shouting and so was Elizabeth. But some one had made a mistake. Mary was still inside. The staircases fell as she ran to them and soon she was in the corner of the bedroom and the flames were creeping across the floor and she was screaming and no-one was listening. The pain ran through her when the first flame licked her, but soon she didn't feel anything any more. She was black and charred and glowing and then breaking and falling and crumbling and then nothing remained.

She woke very early the next morning. It was a clear hard winter's day, and Mary's anger was rough in her throat. She went into the kitchen to set the fire. Liam was sitting at the table cleaning his gun. Mary didn't ask where Elizabeth was. There was no sign of her and there was no sign of Seán. Liam's blue eyes were clear and hard as he looked across at her. "I'm pregnant, Liam," she said. Liam said nothing. "I'm going home for a while. I want to have this baby in peace." Liam said nothing, but he kept his eyes fixed in Mary's. "I think I should tell you who shopped us to the postman," she said after a moment.

Liam stopped working. He said, "Tell me who and

I'll shoot the bastard."

"It was Elizabeth," said Mary, and she saw that Liam was glad. He smiled.

Electricity

Four days before Christmas and the café was hung with paper-chains. Aisling was having her weekly treat, a cup of coffee and a sandwich on her own in town. She was enjoying herself very much. Every now and then she felt for her bag, where her dole and her Christmas bonus lay hidden.

She saw him. He was coming towards her. How long was it. Four years? Eamonn had the darkest hair and the bluest eyes. For four years he had lived in her mythic past, when she was sixteen and everything was new.

He saw her. "Aisling?" He was smiling, she couldn't help smiling back. He really seemed pleased to see her. "You're looking well."

It wasn't true. She looked down.

"What are you doing with yourself these days?"

"Not much."

He smiled. "I don't believe that."

Well, now she'd have to come out with everything. It was always like this. She took a breath and said, "I'm unemployed. It's hard for me to get work. I had a baby a year after…I knew you. I haven't got a chance to go back and do my Leaving since. I can't afford to pay anyone to look after Julie. My mother keeps her

137

one day a week—dole day. I can't ask her to do any more, she's getting on."

She looked up and said strongly, "Julie's lovely. I wouldn't have missed it for the world. I loved the father at the time, but he reacted really badly over me getting pregnant and I soon lost interest in him. I threw him out."

She noticed he was still smiling at her and became embarrassed at the strength of her tone. He didn't need the lecture. He wasn't drawing back. "So what about yourself," she said, to break the silence.

Eamonn smiled. "Oh, you know yourself. I'm between jobs."

They both laughed, and he went on, "I qualified as a teacher... Irish and music. I've never had a full-time job, just the odd few weeks filling in for teachers having babies and broadening their horizons. I love the job, but I suppose I'm going to have to think of something else. I'm still in debt from college."

"You could go to England; they're crying out for teachers there."

"But I don't want to go. I get the impression once I go there it's all over. I'll have to stay, I'll have responsibilities there. Anyway, I don't know why I should." He smiled. "Maybe I'm just too scared."

He seemed different, softer, easier to talk to. Then he'd been a the college student, full of himself and what he was going to do. There hadn't been any place for her in it all. It was just a few weeks one summer. But Aisling had always remembered it carefully as her one real experience of love.

"Will you have another coffee?" he said, and she said yes, and reached for her bag.

"Let me. I got my Christmas bonus today, it's my chance to treat a lady."

Outside the lunchtime shoppers dashed up and down the street, battalions of women in highheels, men with their ties askew and newspapers in their hands. It was four days till Christmas and there was so much to be bought. Aisling and Eamonn were swept along the street by the tides of people and the electricity in the air. They were talking so much they hardly knew where they were. It had been so long since Aisling had talked to another adult, she kept marvelling—he understands! He understood everything, he knew what it was like. They could not keep walking along the street forever, and so they went into a pub and squeezed onto the red velvet seats, ordered hot whiskeys, then more hot whiskeys. Aisling's head was spinning, it could have been the whiskey and it could have been Eamonn.

"It's just the little things," she was explaining, "The sole on a shoe or Julie wanting to go to the pantomime…"

"I know," he said. "You could cope with it for a week, or maybe a fortnight…but then you just say to yourself, I need money, there are all these things just beyond my reach, just a little money and they'd all be mine."

"Everybody else having a decent Christmas, and you stuck in in your tatty old clothes. Who'd look at you anyway?" Aisling was getting tearful and angry, she was on her third whiskey.

Eamonn looked at her hard. He took her hand and said, "I haven't been with anyone in so long."

Aisling met his look and smiled. "Neither have I."

He leant over and kissed her and her body shuddered like an old car. "You know what I'd like to do?" she said, after a moment. "I'd like to have dinner in a restaurant. I've been dreaming of going to a restaurant. As my Christmas treat. To celebrate meeting up with you again."

Because things would be different now. Maybe they could help each other find a job. Give each other strength and confidence. They walked out into the night among the fairy-lights and the shop windows. They had their arms round each other, and every now and then they kissed, and it was warm and soft. They crossed the Liffey and saw a restaurant with candles flickering at the tables and they went in. Eamonn was good at French and he ordered everything that took his fancy, making her laugh with his silly accent.

Aisling stretched back on the chair and gave herself to it. The food and the wine. Eamonn's eyes shining in the candle-light. She could feel her poor old body thawing and opening out again like a flower in water. And she knew her eyes were shining too, she could read it in Eamonn's. They ate as much as they could, until the waiter was laughing with them, and then they had liqueurs and coffee. Aisling touched Eamonn's knee then and said, "Stay with me tonight."

He said "yes" and she handed him her purse and told him to pay half of it, whatever it was, and not to let her know. And then they walked out into the frosty night and up Dame Street towards the house.

It was past midnight when they got back and Julie had been asleep a long time. Aisling touched her cheek and Eamonn smiled at her. Aisling's mother's snores filtered through from the other room and

Aisling felt guilty for leaving her with the child for so long. But it was worth it. She would be better for Julie now, she was happier, not so resentful. They went downstairs and made up a bed on the sitting-room floor and sat a while by the electric fire warming their hands. They began to kiss and they realised how desperately they had needed the comfort of another body. The electric fire lit their smooth young bodies with orange warmth. They made love for a long time, until they were laughing at themselves and the battle between love and exhaustion. Aisling fell asleep with her head somewhere between Eamonn's chin and stomach, and Eamonn fell asleep with his arm around her.

The night hours were still. Stray dogs padded up and down the street sniffing for food. A joyrider tore up the street doing ninety. The night hours were cold. But the electric fire burned on and Aisling and Eamonn slept uncovered. The orange light contended with the dawn for a bit, but presently clean, blue light poured into the room.

Eamonn was dreaming about Aisling, living it through again. He slept deeply and when he woke eventually, shivering with cold, the clock on the mantelpiece said eight o'clock. He had to get out before Aisling's mother came down. He sat up quickly. Aisling wasn't there. He threw on his clothes and went into the kitchen. "Aisling!"

She was sitting with her back to him. She did not turn.

"Aisling, love."

He bent down to kiss her, but then he saw her shoulders were shaking. There was money spread out on the table, neat rows and piles of pounds and pence. She said, very quiet and even, "You didn't tell me how much we spent."

"You asked me not to."

She turned then, furious, "I had no idea. What am I going to do? I have to buy presents, food, shoes, clothes. I have a child to support."

"I'll help you."

"You've got nothing yourself." Eamonn was silent. "It was the end of my Christmas, not the beginning."

"We have each other."

"What good is that. We can't bring Julie to bed with us. Jesus. Jesus."

Then she clenched her fists and roared, "We left the electric fire on all night."

That was the last thing she ever said to him. She put her face down on the table and cried. She lashed out at him if he touched her, and it got late, so in the end he put on his coat and made to leave. He threw a fiver onto the kitchen table,

"For the electricity."

But she turned round and stuffed it in his pocket, shivering with rage. He heard Julie call her mother then, and her quick, bright, hungry step on the stairs. And as there was nothing he could say, he let himself out into the bustling city.

Night Fall

Before night they said they'd come if they were coming. Over the sands in their shiny shoes and new suits to Seán Og's little house by the side of the sea. I remember the first time they came, how many years ago...ten, fifteen? Brought here by Máire Kennedy, anxious to keep them in her little guesthouse. They had their tape-recorders with them, and their little note books. It was years since I'd told a story, but of course I never said that to them. It would be on the radio, they said, I'd make money out of it. And so I fished around in the blackness of my mind until I found the bright thread of a story, and when I pulled, out they spilled, story after story after story.

And now Oisín had been in the land of youth three hundred years and Fionn was dead and the Fianna were dead, and his dog Bran and Sceolong, long dead and buried. And they loved it, oh, they couldn't have enough of it, and Máire Kennedy made tea and handed round pieces of barmbrack until darkness fell and the men went away and all I could see were their flashlights on the sands.

Some time later Máire Kennedy took me up after mass in her great rattling Ford to her neat white guesthouse above the town and lit a great fire for me, and gave me a good dinner, and turned on the radio. And sure enough there I was as clear as a bell. And so Oisín went to Niamh one day and said, Niamh, I have been here living in your love for a long time, and I miss Ireland, I miss my father, my family, the Fianna. And Niamh sighed a deep sigh and said I will get you a horse and you can go to them, but if your foot touches the land of Ireland, you can never return here, you will never see me again.

There I was, and there was Michael Flaherty and Eoin Og, and they wheezing away at their stories, "Did you hear the one about the three-legged goose?" And later there arrived a letter in a thin white envelope, there was such a richness, they said, of oral tradition on the island that they'd decided to organise an annual story-telling festival, bringing people in from all over the world. And they wondered would I be available, and named a sum. Enough to pay for a new suit of clothes and a visit to my sister in Coventry. I said yes and next I got the brochure in the post, and a big picture of myself on the front of it. And Máire Kennedy drove me up to town and I got the suit on tick and said I'd pay it back when the money came through. He agreed immediately, for he'd heard me on the radio and I was as smart as any of them when the day came.

The day came and we sat up on a stage with microphones stuck in front of us, myself, Séamus Og and Michael Flaherty. I was last and I watched the audience as the others spoke, big Dubliners in shiny shoes and yellow-haired young girls. I found myself looking into the blue eyes of a lovely girl and she smiled at me when the man introduced me. I kept my eyes on her as I began to speak. My voice shivered, then it found its strength and I pulled and pulled at the ribbon of stories in my mind, finding a new power and richness in my voice. And so Oisín rode for seven days and seven nights until he reached the shores of Ireland. He followed the curve of rivers and mountains until he reached the land of the Fianna. But the land was deserted. The plain stretched out dark and empty and Oisín's heart grew dark and empty too. He rode on looking about him, but the wind whistled over the dark land, he recognised nothing. I could tell they were enjoying it, for the girl was smiling at me and when I finished there was burst of clapping. Afterwards there was drinking till the small hours, as much as we could hold, and the RTE men kept questioning me up and down where I first heard them and did I know this and that one, and me telling them a pack of lies and them nodding, writing everything down. And the young German girl kissed me as I got into Máire Kennedy's car, sending tingles right down into me, the first time I touched a woman in maybe forty years, since I lost the farm and I lost Mary Kelly to my brother.

Before night they said they'd come if they were coming. I dread the dark, only the one tilly lamp to hold it off, the cold deepening, the silence filling with voices long dead. Is it any wonder I could tell stories, and me talking all day to myself, talking all day to myself, only on mass day I talk to anyone else. They'll hardly come now. I suppose I got careless. I didn't prepare as much as I should have. And Oisín saw an old man pushing a stone along a road and he asked him what had happened to the Fianna, where were

Fionn and his men. And the old man narrowed his weak eyes and said, that was hundreds of years ago, they're dead now and buried and their time is past.

And I must have got distracted by something, I was tugging and tugging at my string of stories but all I could see was blackness, blackness. And Oisín put his hands to his face then and cried for Fionn and the Fianna. And then he turned his horse again towards Niamh and the land of youth. But before he left he reached down from his saddle to move the stone that the old man was pushing...I could go no further. I looked up and saw rows of stone-dead eyes and Máire Kennedy's in the front row, narrowing. One of the RTE people brought me out, gave me a cup of tea, and although I didn't know yet what had happened to me, I began to sob. And the saddle-strap broke and Oisín fell to the ground, and the moment he touched the ground he took on the weight of his years and became a frail old man, near blind, near deaf...and forgetful. Everything that had ever had meaning for him was dead and buried. He could hear no sound. He was terrified. All he could see around him was blackness, like the blackness closing in on me now, as night falls.

Friend

"I want you," she said. She came out of the shadows. She had on a short black skirt. Her breasts were tight little fists under her skimpy jumper. She pushed her long black hair out of her eyes. He didn't think. He moved forward and caught one of those little fists in his. He closed his eyes and they went at it while the printer churned out Colm's advertising copy, "Sauvage...The Scent for the Wild in the Man." It was soon over. The printer stopped and sat quiet, reams of paper hanging limply out of it. She tossed her hair back again and looked at him sideways and he laughed and pulled up his trousers. They both felt very pleased with themselves.

"See you," she said. "Wednesday. The Imperial." He laughed again. It was ludicrous, but good fun. She was very beautiful and he was flattered. She turned and left the printing room and he sat for a few moments before he gathered up his copy. He didn't know if he would keep the appointment or not. He didn't think anything through.

"I want a friend," his wife Maria had said. She was a strange, gawky creature. Few men in her north Mayo hometown could have found her attractive and perhaps that was why she came to rely so fiercely on herself. But she had a special power, the seriousness in her dark eyes. She spoke carefully and slowly and you believed everything she said to you. Colm was fascinated by her from the first few words. He met her when they were both doing Master's theses in poetry in the University of Ulster. He tried to get to know her, but the usual lines didn't seem to have any effect, she would just look at him oddly. Then he was left in Portrush in the rain for the Easter weekend. He met her on the street and asked her for coffee. And he found himself talking with an openness never before experienced. It was her quiet smile and her slow speech. He trusted her. They talked until one in the morning and he expected to go to bed with her…that was the routine. But she didn't seem to think of it and he was too shy to suggest it. He wondered did she have someone else, was she gay, paranoid? They spent the Sunday together and the Monday and then he started to read her his poetry. He finished a poem and looked up for her reaction and she reached out and touched him, touched him somewhere new, secret and tender. She released him like hundreds of old carpets flung over balconies in summer. They lay in each other's warmth at four in the morning and Colm asked, "Do you ever want to get married, Maria?"

And she said, "I want a friend."

Colm was radiant with love and he wanted to proclaim it to the world. Getting married was his idea. She wasn't much interested. She took him for granted, but with the fiercest passion. She trusted him totally and her happiness was a soft, deep fire. They had a baby, Katrina; she was four now. Maria loved her child, but she was not possessive. She taught part-time and wrote poetry in the afternoons. Colm left academia, with its endless one-year contracts, and started his own advertising agency in Dublin. He was a very successful, beautiful young man of thirty-two. Women noticed him.

He spent his days in the world of power, the world of profit and loss. At night he came home to his still, passionate wife. For Maria, money was a substance which bought you the things you needed, whereas increasingly for Colm, it came to mean personal success. He began to crave from her the adulation he got from the women in the office, but it just wasn't there. Then subtly, he began to try to make her possessive of him. "I have a new secretary, Fiona. Pretty woman, has a degree in French and Italian. Very pretty woman."

Maria would smile and say something off the point, like had she spent much time on the continent. Colm would wrench the conversation round.

"She's not married. At least, she's divorced. She was married in France, you see. Amazing for a woman that young to have been through so much!"

And concern, that was what Maria would show! Concern for the woman's happiness! He sometimes wondered had she been reared by spirits in her isolated north Mayo home. She seemed to ignore the conventions of sexuality. She felt no jealousy. But she was as warm, as sensual, as ever before and her mind was a garden of colours and words. He knew he was the luckiest man alive and he whispered "I love you!" into her ear in bed. She never replied, but she squeezed him tight and smiled. He was her friend.

He would lie on the pristine hotel linen and run his fingers down Fiona's brown body, over the muscles she pumped up at the company gym. They did everything they should and there was nothing wrong with it, and yet Colm wondered just why... what... Fiona was thirty-five now, her husband had left her for a twenty-year old. Success meant everything to her. She could feel Colm thinking about Maria and jealousy grew up in her like a sickly plant. She redoubled her efforts, arranged lunches, after-noons...even a weekend. She wanted to beat Maria, and she knew the first step was to make her jealous. Then there would be a show-down. Then decisions would have to be made.

Maria was not beautiful. That was the only fact Fiona registered when she first saw her at the office party. Fiona grew tall. She flounced into the room and seemed to take it over, beaming lipstick into every corner. She had built Maria into something quite different from this small dark woman, dressed in brown and looking her age. She was surprised that Colm could have married someone so lacking in sex-appeal. She kept smiling over at Colm, but he didn't seem to notice her, he was bending over his wife, touching her. Fiona circled closer and suddenly she began to see a sort of power in Maria. What was it...? Something outside her experience. A sort of in-dependence. She didn't need Colm as much as Fiona did. They stood together and yet Maria stood separate in the halo of her originality. And when Fiona followed Colm and tried to kiss him in the foyer, he winced away.

"What's wrong?" she said.

He laughed and leaned forward, gave her a peck on the cheek. And then he went back into the buffet room and back to his wife.

The jealousy grew stronger and sicker in Fiona. She drove herself home and flung herself into bed, sick with what she called love. How could Colm ignore her after all the afternoons, the days? How could he insult her? Keeping up a front of the perfect marriage and having his bit on the side all the same. She was not going to be undervalued like this, alright for a bit of fun, but not the sort of woman you were serious about. Maria would have to find out about it, that was all. Fiona turned on the bedside lamp and found a pen and paper.

Dear Maria, she wrote, I have been having an affair with your husband for three months. Colm is too frightened to tell you, but when I met you tonight I decided you were too lovely a person to be deceived in this way. Love never follows our plans for it. I don't know how it began, but there's no going back now. We didn't choose to fall in love. I can imagine the effect these words are having on you...I know what it's like. But I wonder is it really better to go on living a lie? You are young enough to be able to make a new life, this time without a lie in it. I am feeling your pain as much as you. Yours with affection, Fiona Davis.

Her hands were shaking as she put the letter into the envelope. She dropped it into the outgoing mail the next morning before she could have second thoughts. If Colm saw it, he probably thought it was an invitation to a dinner party.

A day passed and Maria was wandering around the house with a cup of coffee, letting words and rhythms shift in her mind and smiling to herself. She saw the letter on the hall mat. She picked it up and opened it. She began to read. Her throat was dry. She sat down and tried to focus. Her certainty, her confidence. Colm was her friend. They were bound together by a thousand filaments, like branches grafted together. Maria let out a long wail of pain and lay back on the chair. She lay there with her long, lonely wails for some time.

She didn't feel anger. Just bewilderment and pain. It was five o'clock and Maria roused herself and hurried to buy food before Katrina was brought home. The car nosed its way to the supermarket like an old dog. The shop suited her mood in an odd way, the piped music, the cold light and shining surfaces. She tossed things into her basket and made her way to the cashier. Five thirty-five and a woman was passing through the check-out several people ahead of Maria. Her scarf flapped as she walked now, Coco Chanel. Maria threw down her basket and followed her into the car-park. Fiona got into her car and tried to shut the door, but Maria grabbed it and held it open.

"Stop!"

"Leave me alone!"

"We need to talk."

"Yes. You must. I don't understand."

It was beginning to rain and Fiona leant over and opened the passenger door. Two lovely women in their thirties. They looked at each other.

"I got the letter."

"Good. You understand then." Fiona kept her eyes in front of her. There was a pause.

Then Maria said, "No."

"What?"

"I don't understand."

"What can I say to you?"

"Please..."

Maria was crying. Fiona looked at her quickly. She clenched her hands on the wheel and bit her lip. Maria said, "Why?"

"Does anyone know why they do anything?"

"They should."

"It's happened. I'm sorry."

"What is it you want from him?"

Fiona almost laughed. She held out her hands to enclose the silent everything and nothing.

"Well..."

"What?"

"Love!"

"You love each other?"

"It's physical. Sex."

"Sex?"

"Don't you know what that is?"

"Colm and I made love this morning. I still feel warm."

Maria was silent for a moment. Then, "He wants to leave me and Katrina just for sex?"

"What else?"

"Please...I want to understand. It'd be different if our relationship had changed or gone cold...Well, of course we'd split up. But it didn't seem as if anything had changed. And if he felt differently, why didn't he tell me? How could he lie to me? He's my best friend, we've been together for ten years."

Fiona winced, but Maria went on, "I still feel warm from him this morning."

"Stop!"

Maria looked up. Fiona's eyes were burning. "Stop that!"

Maria said nothing.

"I'd prefer you to scream! I can cope with that. I've seduced other men before. But Colm was different, because I was never important to him."

Maria reached out and touched her, but she went on savagely, "That's all I wanted, but I didn't get it. That letter was rubbish and the whole affair was...nothing. It's just sometimes I feel so worthless, I have to put something into my life. I don't think I have any real friends. My women friends hate me because they fear me. And I hate them."

Suddenly she laughed and looked at Maria, who smiled. Fiona went quiet and looked at Maria a moment. "You're a lovely woman. So calm and gentle and intelligent. So beautiful."

Sleet hammered against the car and they sat there, quiet. And Maria wondered how she would ask Colm why people who don't lie to friends lie to lovers.

Eva

Turloch ground his teeth and grunted and grunted again and Alison felt a rush inside her. She stared out through the chink in the curtain. It was early morning, but already a thick coal-smog had claimed the city. Turloch moved over and snored lightly. For a week now they had known she was pregnant and he had had sex with her every morning since. There was no messing about with condoms or anything of course, and he woke for his feed as regularly as a baby. Before they had known she was pregnant he had only had sex with her once. It was behind the fruit-machines. It was three in the morning and everyone else had gone home, except Pat, who must have known what Turloch was about, and hung around the back conveniently for long enough.

"Come on," Turloch said.

She screamed "No!" but he hit her, he brought her down. And she went quiet. It was like when she was a child and she held out her hand for her mother to slap her. It hurt no more and it didn't last much longer. There was this wet feeling between her legs and then on her face. "Christ, I'm sorry," he was saying, crying like a child. She was seventeen. She had been a virgin. She said nothing, and he pulled her clothes around her hurriedly. Afterwards she saw her tights were in ribbons and her bra straps were broken. He drove her home in his gleaming Japanese car, and never said a word to her all the way. She felt a dumb ache in her stomach but she told no-one and she went into work the next day. He never as much as went near her until she told him she was pregnant. She felt a dumb ache about that too; the only thing that panicked her was telling her parents.

The noises of the amusement arcade rose in prominence now, a medley of computer yelps and rubber balls. It wasn't the sort of place her mother would have wanted her to work, and Alison lied feebly, said she worked in a shop. Her mother guessed something was up, but she said nothing. She was glad of the few quid Alison contributed. Alison was intelligent, could have gone to college, but somehow she had lacked the energy to fill in the forms and enter the race. She was pretty too, small and pale, with wispy fair hair and a freckly face. She would often gaze at herself in the mirror after she'd put on her make-up, because she hardly recognised the image.

Alison's father hardly counted any more. He was so weak since he lost the job. He kept up a front of perfect politeness, he dressed well in his business suit. He seemed to say, I am clean, at least, I am well-educated. Overlook me and tolerate me even if I have failed. Even if I have failed you. All I need is the edge of a crust and a space to lie down quietly and respectably, and die. Mrs Doherty went to confession every week, whispered her sins through the iron grille, whispered her sins, whatever they were. What sins could a woman like Mrs Doherty have? Mr. Doherty didn't go to confession and Mrs Doherty's whisperings were a constant reproach to him. He was guilty of plunging the family into its present economic chaos after all, and it was getting more and more difficult to keep up the payments on the house. It was all such a weight and it bore down on Alison. She listened to the silences and the whispering and felt frightened and guilty, but she didn't know why and she didn't know what to do.

Turloch's mouth was open. He was very tall and quite plump, he was very pale. He was all choked up with smoking. He had a wife and child somewhere in the suburbs. He hated them. He was going to get an annulment, he said, he was going to marry Alison. He was twenty years older than she was but he clung to her. They smoked their cigarettes together nervously, they went through with sex as if it were the cruellest penance in God's creation, and the pregnancy was a part of that penance. They would have the child and they would stay together. They did not consider an abortion.

Alison got up and washed as well as she could at the sink. She parted her hair at the speckled mirror and brushed it out. She didn't look too bad. She didn't look any different. So much had happened in the last few weeks but an innocent young face still looked out at Alison. On Wednesdays Alison went to see her grandmother and she always tried to make herself look nice. Her grandmother was a fine old lady who lived in a Victorian square in leafy south Dublin. For Alison she had always been a small, neat smiling woman in a twin-set and pearls, first flanked by a tall, black-suited husband, now alone. But there were stories about Eva, about her stint in art college, her campaigns for conservation, socialised medicine and women's rights. And there were photographs too, of a beautiful woman in a brocaded kaftan, of a bride with her ankles on show. Grandad Quinlan had married her for her beauty, which had not faded even now. Alison was pleased that everyone said she took after her grandmother. She would have loved to have been more like her in spirit too, but that was impossible now. In her grandmother's eyes she had not changed, however, and Alison wanted to conceal the pregnancy from her as long as possible. To her grandmother she was still a young girl with everything before her, whereas it was all very much behind her now. The idyllic garden days of rounders and high tea vanished with grandad's death and granny's age, but still it was a temporary heaven to sit at granny's fire and drink tea out of delicate china cups. Alison beat the shadow over her grandmother's life to the edges of her consciousness.

Now she walked up the granite steps and rang the bell and her grandmother opened, pink and smiling, her hair hammered into her head with a hundred hairpins. The fire was lighting and the tea things were set out and Alison sat down. Her grandmother poured the tea and they sipped and talked back and forth about boyfriends Eva had had when she was Alison's age. It all seemed so romantic, all magic lanterns and boxes of chocolates.

"Do you still have the same boyfriend, Alison?"
"Yes."
"What's his name?"

"Turloch."

"That's a strange name. It must be some sort of an Irish name. Is he good to you?"

Alison buried her head in her knees a second and said, "Yes."

"Don't go getting married yet, love. You've plenty of time."

"I know, Gran."

"No matter how much you love him."

The light was fading. They talked back and forth and then Eva said, "I saw my doctor the other day" and Alison looked up.

"Things aren't as good as they were."

"What do you mean?"

"You know. I have to be ready. I want to tell you something first. I've never told this to anyone before. I don't want it to die with me." She hesitated, then, "It was my words killed your grandfather."

"What?"

Blackness, blackness, all over everything, running through everything. Was there nothing clean? Alison wanted to cover her ears, to shout, "Don't go any further!" but instead she bit her lip and clenched her hands on the chair.

"I got angry with him, Alison. There had been years and years of lies. He was so afraid of himself. I would try to talk things through, but he would head off into his own wilderness of little lies. Lies about business, lies about friendship, lies about love."

Eva looked at Alison and Alison tightened her hands on the chair.

"I felt raw love for him in the beginning. But in those days you didn't see too much of some one before you married and so I didn't realise he didn't have that kind of love for me. His love was already fettered by some guilt in him. He snatched love in the dark when he thought no-one could see him, and then trembled because he knew he'd been seen. So my love stopped. But he wouldn't listen to me. He pretended it wasn't happening. I was pregnant and I stayed with him... lying on the other side of that bed, dead as doornails. I never should have stayed, but at the time I worried it might kill him if I left. I shouldn't have worried. I should have just gone. It's no wonder he developed a heart condition, with all that fear bottled up inside. He sat there, day after day, terrified of dying. A man nearly sixty! I was breaking, Alison. He was ordering me all over town. He kept in touch with his office by telephone. They didn't clear his desk. It went on for two months like that. He was going downhill, and his face had a scandalised look on it, as if to say...how could this happen to me? One day I asked the doctor what to expect, and he told me I'd better start making arrangements. I went to my husband, and he was sitting up in bed. Maybe he'd heard something, he was as white as a sheet. He asked me what the doctor had said, and his eyes pleaded with me, lie to me! I'd gone along with him all my life. But now I had knowledge and he asked me for it. I thought it was time we became adults. I took his hand and said, "The doctor says you don't have much time, Johnny."

But maybe we weren't ready. He turned his face from me and said, 'Nonsense, Eva. I feel better today. You're talking nonsense!'

"The fear boiled up inside him. He died of it that night. His dead eyes looked...scandalised. The eyes of a scandalised baby."

Alison was struggling in the words, but she could find no plank, no land.

"You don't understand, I can see it in your face," said Eva.

"Why did you have to tell me?"

"I wanted you to understand."

"Oh, I forgive you..."

"It's not forgiveness I need. I thought you'd understand. Instead you make a judgement on me."

"I've enough trouble of my own at the moment..." The tears overflowed down Alison's face.

"What, love? Perhaps I can help."

"It's not something I want to talk about."

"What hope have any of us if we don't share our troubles? I'd feel privileged if you'd let me help."

"I don't want help, right? Forget I said anything. Please, Gran."

There was a moment. Alison felt the tea-pot should explode, the tea-cups shatter, but nothing happened, the flames threw their shapes as quietly as before. Then Eva said, "I'm very tired and I'd like you to leave."

She stood up and Alison stood up too. Then she leant forward her cheek and Alison kissed it. She walked into the hall and Alison followed her and went out. She turned and saw her grandmother lit up in the chink and she said, "See you next Wednesday."

Her grandmother nodded once silently and shut the door.

***

It was dark and Alison walked quickly along the canal. "It was my words killed your grandfather." It had happened when Alison was a child. She had enough trouble already. How dare her grandmother make her suffer like this? Well-to-do Dublin dribbled out to nothing. The air grew thick with fumes from the brewery. The derelict sites off Clanbrassil Street were dark and empty except for the orange pool of a huge bonfire lighting up a circle of young faces, mesmerised by the one colourful thing in sight. Everything was sodden, dirty. There was nothing she could do about it, it had gone wrong long before she was born. She reached the cathedral and found she was crying, but she didn't bother wiping her face because it had started to drizzle. Her jacket drank it in and she felt cold. She walked on, down the winding streets towards the amusement arcade. It was dark inside except for the lights on the machines. Warlord, Spacebuster. The figures did not turn to look. She went upstairs, still shaking from her tears, took off her wet clothes and put on her dressing-gown. She made tea and toast and was still sitting eating at the table when Turloch came in. He gave her a look.

"What's wrong with you?"

"Nothing."

" Did you see your gran? Is she not well?"

"No, Turloch, she's grand."

Turloch sat down. "What's wrong, love?"

His sympathy moved her and she could feel tears coming on again. "Everything seems so black, somehow."

"Don't worry, love."

Turloch leaned forward and it was then Alison saw her wrap had come away and her leg was bare. Turloch touched her and looked at her. Then he moved his hand up her leg and Alison said, "No, Turloch, not now."

Turloch's hand slipped up further and Alison said firmly, "No."

"Come on," he said, and put his arm round her. She felt too weak to try any more, she let him do what he liked. Afterwards she rolled towards the wall and wouldn't speak and so Turloch turned on the television. Alison looked at the shapes on the wall. She would have to stop this, she would have to change things. The next day she would tell her parents about the pregnancy. She would clean the room out, change the sheets. She would bring Turloch's jeans to the launderette. She would not see her grandmother for some time.

***

"Is he going to marry you, that's what I want to know."

"He would if he could."

"What do you mean, he would if he could? What's stopping him?"

"He was married before."

"He was married before. Oh, now it comes out. What happened to his wife?"

"They never see each other. It never worked out at all. Turloch's hoping for an annulment."

"That's how he pulled the wool over your eyes. Gracious God, I thought I had you better brought up."

Alison's mother faced her over the table. Her father held her hand, and suddenly he said, with only pity in his voice, "You're so young, Alison!"

Alison's mother continued quickly, "We'll have to hope to heaven the annulment comes through, or have an illegitimate child on our hands. It's all I needed now, what with Gran so ill, but I have to say I'm not surprised. What do you have to say for yourself?"

Alison said she was sorry. She could think of nothing else.

"Have you thought out what's going to happen if he doesn't get an annulment? How are you going to support the child?"

"Turloch will support me."

"You'll have to put it in for adoption, that's what. I suppose we'll have to put you into one of those pricey homes. It's all we needed now, with Dad out of work."

Mrs Doherty started to cry, and Alison looked on in horror. She had done this, it was her fault. Mrs Doherty finished crying and looked steadily at Alison. "The least you can do for me now is go to confession this evening. That's the least you can do."

The shutter scraped back. It was the young priest who had prepared them for confirmation. He had blue eyes and a beard and he looked like Christ. The whole class had fancied him.

"Bless me father," she began with a start, "for I have sinned. It is one year since my last confession."

Her voice was shaking, she was sure he recognised it, but his fine profile revealed nothing.

"What sins have you to confess?" he asked.

The words seemed too big to come out.

"I'm pregnant, father."

His Adam's apple moved, his lips tightened. "Are

you married?"

"No, father."

Alison started to cry, but she went through with it, yes father, I am heartily sorry, father. Thou art infinitely good, father. I will never offend Thee again, father.

"Your penance will go on for the rest of your life. Whenever you look at that child you will remember it was a child conceived in sin, in weakness. But you must love it all the same, for it is God's child."

"Yes, father."

"I absolve you," he said finally, but then he said, "Remember, only Christ can look into your heart and see if the sin is truly repented."

And Alison felt her heart open as easily as a ripe melon, ripe and rotten. She could hardly walk down the road with it, it was so heavy.

***

She couldn't face going home and she knew it would be wrong, anyhow. She would go back to Turloch. They would wait for the baby, they would wait for the annulment. She would not let him near her again until after they were married. She pressed the door open. As usual the figures at the machines did not move. Upstairs Turloch was sitting on the bed eating a sandwich. When Alison came in he looked up.

"Where were you?"

"Turloch," she said. "I told my parents."

Turloch paled. Then he said, "What did they say?"

"My mother went mad. She told me to go to confession."

"Did you go?"

"Yes."

Turloch looked down, as if he thought the priest might know him.

"I want to change things between us," she went on. "I don't want us to…do it until the annulment comes through. It's not right to go on the way we're going. I'm sick with it."

Turloch's sandwich lay uneaten on his lap. He said, "The annulment?"

"So that we can get married. So that we can be parents to the child."

Turloch looked towards Alison's stomach. He put his hands over his face and sat there a long time saying nothing. Alison began cleaning the room, and it got dark and neither of them turned on the light. Turloch looked odd, sitting like that and Alison began to feel lonely.

"Turloch," she said, but he shook his head, he didn't say anything. "Turloch!"

The television was burbling and Alison turned it off and got into her nightdress. She felt very alone, suddenly. She went over and shook Turloch by the shoulder and said, "Are you coming to bed?"

He nodded and took off his clothes and lay down beside Alison. He seemed exhausted and he slept almost immediately. Alison lay awake. She felt afraid when she thought back over it all, her mother's face, the priest's voice. Most of all she felt afraid when she thought of the baby. She hadn't really thought clearly about it before. A new life growing in her. She felt frightened when she thought about the future. For the first time she wanted his arms around her. She poked him, but he didn't waken. She had to poke him again. He lifted his face from the sheet, and it looked like the face of a stranger.

"What's wrong?"

"Put your arms around me, I'm frightened."

Turloch hesitated, then did as she said. She took his arms and drew them tighter around her. Then she rested his palm flat on her stomach a minute. Suddenly he took his arms away and sat up. "Stop it, Alison! I'm more scared than you, you know."

Alison sat up too, and faced him in the dark. He was rigid and cold.

"Why, Turloch?"

"I don't want to turn out like my father. He had another family in Cork."

"You never told me."

"We didn't find out for a long time. I'll never forget what my mother went through. He used hit her but she wouldn't cry, she'd just say, 'Stop it, Thomas, stop it!' My mother was a saint. She's looking down at me now. I'm ashamed of myself."

"She'd want you to do your best for me."

"That child should never have been conceived. It's the same as myself and Pauline, that should never have been either. That was wrong. We weren't married either. We should have given the baby up for adoption, but she wouldn't do it, she wouldn't let the baby go. She wanted the baby. See how it's all gone rotten and it's created more sin, and that's created more sin in turn. Myself and Pauline split up, I tried to change, until you came to work here, and you were so pretty. It can't go on, Alison. You'll give the baby up for adoption and we'll go our separate ways and we'll start over again."

"We can't just pretend it hasn't happened..."

"Why not? We can begin again."

Turloch took Alison's hand. "You're a good girl, Alison, but us being together like this is wrong, I can see that clearly now. I didn't know what I was doing before, but I've got to stop it all before it's too late."

He smiled and gripped her hand, but she took it away.

"Do you see that?" he said.

"Yes," she said, but she wasn't really answering his question. He smiled and gripped her hand. Then he closed his eyes and seemed to fall asleep. How could he just turn over and go to sleep, leaving her with all the pain and guilt? Anger swelled up in Alison, for the first time. She put her hands to her stomach and shouted silently, no, no, no! The hours slipped away and she tossed in the bed. The windows whitened. She was all clenched up with anger and resentment and she began to cry then, not with pain, but with anger, anger, anger. Suddenly the phone sprang to life. Alison scrambled over Turloch, threw her dressing-gown on and pawed at the receiver. The phone fell off the table.

"Hello?"

"Alison? It's your mother. I thought you might like to know that your grandmother's much weaker, she's in hospital."

"She's weaker?"

"We've been up all night."

"What hospital?"

"The Meath."

"How is she? What do the doctors think?"

"They don't think there's much time."

Her mother seemed to enjoy saying it, and then Alison understood why. Of course! Because it was Alison's fault. It was Alison's fault for getting pregnant. Alison hardened her voice.

"When can I go and see her?"

"This morning, if you get a chance."

"I'm sure I'll be able to make the time."

"I thought I'd better let you know."

"Yes. Thanks."

"Give her my love when you see her. Myself and Dad are going to bed now."

"I will. Thanks."

"Goodbye, then."

"Bye."

Turloch was sitting up in bed now, blinking at her.

"What's that?"

"My grandmother's dying."

Turloch couldn't take it in. He blinked again and lay down.

***

Alison was calm. She washed and put on her clothes, tried to make herself look as well as she could. Then she went downstairs through the silent games room and out into the fresh morning. The sky was high and blue, the clouds seemed painted on with a soft brush. It was one of those mornings the city hardly seemed to deserve. Alison found fifty pence and went into a coffee shop. She drank her coffee looking out the window. Then she bought grapes, lots of them, although she knew her grandmother probably wouldn't want to eat them. She felt there was some clarification waiting just ahead of her, and she felt ready to understand it. Eva Quinlan was lying against her pillow when Alison came in, and her eyes were closed. Her hair was out of its bun in a white spray around her head and her face was pink.

Alison said, "Gran!" and Eva opened her eyes. Alison went to the side of the bed and sat down and they looked at each other.

"How do you feel, Gran?"

"They have me full of drugs. I don't feel anything."

Tears pricked Alison's eyes. Eva said, "What's wrong?"

"No, nothing. I'm sorry about the other day."

"I'm sorry too. I think I expected too much."

"I don't."

They smiled at eachother. Then Eva said, "What's wrong, Alison?"

Alison knew not to lie. "I'm pregnant, Gran."

Eva took her hand. "Do you love him?"

"He's…he's all I have."

"You didn't plan it."

"No…no…it was the first time…it happened."

"You wanted him to be the first."

Alison started to hurt for her own innocence.

"No…he decided…"

"He what?"

"He took me."

"What do you mean?"

"He raped me!"

"My poor…"

"He raped me!"

"Alison!"

"I'm frightened. I don't know what to do. I don't want it."

"Does he want it?"

"No. He wants me to put it in for adoption and we can go our separate ways."

"He doesn't want you any more."

"He thinks his mother's looking down on him and can see him."

"He sounds sick."

"I hate him. I hate what's inside me. There's a bit of him inside me, and I can't stand it. I don't know where to go. I can't go home, and I won't go back to Turloch."

"Don't go near him again. Live in my house. I won't be going back there. Take the key from my handbag and as much money as you need. Remember, Alison, you're not guilty of anything."

Anger welled up in Alison. She had been raped. She was seventeen. It was so sick the small operation in Britain looked like a cleansing ritual. Eva seemed tired now, and she lay back and closed her eyes. Alison sat on until the nurses started to shoo her away. She waited until they had turned their backs and she opened her grandmother's handbag and took the key and a great wad of money. She kissed her grandmother and went out onto the street.

***

She felt pain for her grandmother, but most of all she felt pain for herself. It made her sick to think how she had been treated and how confused she had been. Her head was spinning, there was a crippling pain in her abdomen, but she had freedom and she would hold on to it. She got back to the old house and climbed the granite steps. It took her ages to get the key to work, there was a knack of turning and pulling. But then it opened. Inside the house was dark and cold. It shocked Alison that her mother should already have cleaned up so thoroughly. The fridge was dark and empty, but Alison felt too sick to go out and find food. And so she made up her grandmother's big bed and lay down on it. Her head was spinning and she had a crippling pain in her abdomen, and yet there were the beginnings of a joy in her. Perhaps it was because of this that she slept longer than she had in days.

The clock-radio was unplugged and all the wind-up clocks had wound down. Alison woke the next day, hungry and sick and with no idea how long she had slept. She went downstairs and looked desperately through the empty cupboards, but there was nothing to eat. She was simply too sick to go out and there was no-one she could phone. She went into the sitting-room hoping there she might find some chocolates, and found a tin of Turkish Delight. Then she noticed the drink was still there—her mother didn't touch the stuff and would hardly bring it home to be a temptation to her father. And so Alison put a bottle of vodka under her arm and brought it back up to bed with the remains of the Turkish Delight.

She thought it might kill the pain and it did a little. She took long gulps of vodka and began not to taste it at all. She gobbled up the last of the Turkish Delight. The light faded and she slept on and off, and then the pain in her abdomen come on again, and she drank more vodka. She must have slept for a while, and when she woke the sun was throwing shapes on the wallpaper, and she became aware of something sounding in the distance. The phone. She got out of bed and was dizzy, fell against the commode. But then she righted herself again and remembered, it was in the dining-room. She ran downstairs and took up the receiver but then she realised that she needn't have done so at all, because she knew who was on the line and she knew why.

"Mother."

"Alison? We didn't know where to find you. How long have you been there?"

"I don't know."

"What's wrong with you? Are you sick or something?"

"No."

Her mother paused for effect and then said, "Your grandmother died this morning."

Alison said nothing, but a peace came over her. It was right. It was time. "Fergal and Ruth are coming in this evening, they're staying with Mary, and Rosemary and John will be staying in your old room. Is that alright?"

Alison said nothing.

"I know what you're worrying about, Alison, but I'm not going to say a thing. I think they've enough to worry about already. Alright?"

"Alright."

"You could get mass and confession in half-an-hour at Gerard's. Myself and Dad could pick you up at Gran's afterwards. I'd like you to go, Alison. For Gran."

In half-an-hour, Alison thought, she would be on her way to England.

"That's fine," she said savagely.

"See you then."

"Yes."

Alison put down the phone. She felt dizzy and sat for a moment, thinking, but then she got to her feet again and up the stairs to her grandmother's room. She put on her clothes and took up her bag. She paused for a moment to smooth her hair at her grandmother's dressing-table mirror. The girl in the glass was pale and bedraggled, a stranger. But she smiled. She went downstairs and out the door and shut it behind her. It gave her some satisfaction that her parents would not be able to get in, would not know where she was.

The church came into view and a resolution formed in her. She would go to confession, alright. She wanted to tell that priest what he could do with his absolution. She wasn't sinful. You made decisions, didn't you? You tried to be adult about those decisions. If you did something you regretted later, you tried to make amends. Or you became the victim of other people's anger for the wrong you'd done. But it wasn't as if there was some black substance which spilled over everything and didn't wash out, even generations later. That was just something made up to keep us in line. That was just something made up to weaken the anger in us for the wrongs we suffered. The world was divided up into the people who buckled under their guilt and the people who knew they needed their anger. Who knew they needed truth and knowledge. Yes. That was it. That was what she would tell him. She joined the long line of aged and middle-aged women on the wooden bench. They stared at her and she smiled back. She was dizzy and weak, but strangely exuberant. She felt a seepage from her, and suddenly, softly, she swam out of consciousness. The bench fell, the women shrieked, "Father, she's afther faintin'!" The priest came flapping from his box. But Alison was deaf to them, lying on the marble floor as if it were a soft bed and smiling to herself.

The Pilgrim

It was no subject for a young man, my family had said. History of Art! Ridiculous. Much better to do business, or accountancy, something that would set me up for life. They were paying, after all. I had given in. It had seemed so much easier. And in return they had given me a holiday in Rome, two weeks to explore the art treasures. I had chosen to go alone, it had seemed romantic. So here I was in a *pensione* on top of a bar near the station.

In the Sistine chapel, to the left of the altar, there's a picture of a woman looking into a mirror. The woman has a strong face, both angular and fleshy and her pale blonde hair is pulled back in a delicate chignon. When I saw Madeleine that first morning, I was startled, because she was identical to Michelangelo's image. I had left my book of plates open at it the night before. She was hardly beautiful, I admit, but she was striking. Madeleine stood out on that shabby verandah in her silk dress and elegant shoes, her eyes closing sleepily like a cat's.

She fascinated me. I suppose I was ripe for being fascinated. I think I had expected to fall in love with a strange, distant, older woman in Rome. Rome fascinated me, and she was like Rome, soft, colourful, sensuous, feminine and slightly decayed. It took me a day to get lonely. There was an ache inside me, an ache to share my impressions with some one else. But I spoke no Italian and I disdained to talk to the blue-eyed American rich kids who went to expensive schools. And so, sullenly, I did my round of the sights, and rang home whenever my pride let me.

At night I would see Madeleine in the dining-room, her imperturbable Madonna's face. I wondered what she could be doing there. Resting up after an illness? Or did she just find it a convenient place to live? Did she have a man somewhere, was she looking for one? She was probably in her late thirties, much too young for a woman to forget about love.

Signora Amalfi was not doing great business, although it was August, and so I was surprised when I saw the little tour bus outside the *pensione* one evening. From the south, said the Signora, her eyebrows arching towards her hair-line. "They are coming to see the pope!" When I entered the dining-room I saw all the tables and chairs had been pushed together for the group, except for a single table in the corner. And so, heavy with embarrassment, I went to sit beside Madeleine.

I smiled exaggeratedly as I sat down. Excuse me, may I, I have no alternative, I was saying. A ripple went over her face, and she nodded her head. Then her eyes met mine and she said, "You're from Ireland, aren't you?"

I couldn't speak for a moment. It wasn't just that she spoke English. Her accent was as Irish as mine.

"I see you're surprised."

"I didn't know you were Irish."

"Don't I look Irish?"

Of course she did. I felt slightly disappointed. I much preferred the idea of a distant, foreign woman.

"What's your name?" I asked and she said "Madeleine," and smiled. And when I looked at her again her magic had come back for me. Madeleine was magnificent.

It had been a week since I'd had a chance to talk and the floodgates opened. I told her everything. I told her all about my parents' ignorant attitude to art. When I look back I realise that she told me almost nothing about herself, just that she was living permanently in Rome, living permanently with Signora Amalfi. She liked it in Rome, she said, and I had no difficulty understanding that. Obviously the explanation was thin, but I was too shy to ask her direct questions about herself. And I don't think I wanted to hear answers anyway, I wanted her as a character in my story, not in one of her own. We sat on the terrace in the thick Roman night, talking against the clatter of the pilgrims from Palermo. And before we retired to our rooms, she had promised to come on a walk with me the next morning.

The night was particularly hot, I remember, and I kicked the sheets off me. The Roman adventure was beginning. Madeleine was beautiful and as lonely as I was. There was no reason why I shouldn't take her hand. I think I was confused in my mind at this stage. I didn't know if Madeleine was flesh or painted by Michelangelo, I didn't make any connection between the person I was in Rome and the person I was in Dublin. The heat, the foreignness, made me strange to myself.

We set off after coffee, the Piazza di Spagna, Shelley and Keats's house, the Cafe Greco. We talked about Rome, about Signora Amalfi. Madeleine asked about Ireland, what the weather had been like, what the economy was doing. It was the soda bread she missed most of all, she said. That and the tea. Finally I asked, "Are you working here, Madeleine?"

She smiled a tight smile. "I haven't had to yet. I have money…of my own. Maybe later on I'll go back to nursing, if they let me in here, of course. I keep telling myself I'll have to do some voluntary work, helping unmarried mothers or something."

She said "unmarried mothers" with a faint wince, I thought. It was possible she was an orthodox Catholic. But when I looked at her face, that didn't disturb me a bit. It suited her stillness, her paleness.

Soon the sun got too hot and we cowered under vine leaves in a trattoria. The food rolled over my taste buds and sun dappled Madeleine's hair. The wine made us merry, even Madeleine became giggly. I was deliciously happy, every sense dilated and gratified.

"Funny both of us ending up in Signora Amalfi's, and not speaking to each other for a week."

Madeleine smiled and said yes.

"Do you know many people here?" I asked

"No. I know no-one," she said and looked away.

The wine was making me maudlin. "It's funny, Rome was lost on me, because I had no one to share it with. Don't you find that?"

"I'm used to it, I suppose."

"You don't mind showing me round like this?"

"Not at all."

She smiled again, this time into my face. Suddenly,

I reached for her hand, just to squeeze it, to seal some kind of partnership, but her hand retreated under the table, a frightened animal.

"I didn't...I said.

"I know, I know."

She composed her face into a tinny smile.

"We'd better pay this and get on to St Peter's, I suppose."

I pulled a large pink note out of my pocket. I wouldn't let her pay. I was angry, but it was only an anger I trumped up to cover my desolation and embarrassment.

Somehow we got ourselves onto a bus and into the all-embracing arms of St Peter's Square. I don't know what we were talking about, but we kept some sort of noise going between us. We were entering the great womb of St Peter's when I noticed her voice was stretched out and snapping, when I noticed tears in her eyes. She stopped suddenly, so that the crowd had to fork and surge around her.

"I'm sorry," she said.

I wanted to touch her, to comfort her, but I stayed my hand. She hurried to the side and up the aisle, and I followed her. She knelt on a bench with streaming eyes looking upwards. "We'd been on holiday on the coast, myself, my husband and the kids."

I sank back on the seat and held my breath.

"I don't know how it happened, but the travel agency got our tickets mixed up. When we got to the airport we discovered there were only three seats booked. Of course we were horrified, but it was the high season, there were no cancellations. The children were due in school the next day, David was due in the office. So I volunteered to stay over and get a flight as soon as the agency could find one. I kissed my kids goodbye; I kissed my husband goodbye. I didn't fancy the airport hotel where the agency was going to put me up and so I took a train into town and booked into Signora Amalfi's. I decided to make the most of the mistake, and I headed straight for St Peter's.

"It was the first time I'd been in a strange place on my own, perhaps ever. It was an odd feeling, a free feeling. I was enjoying myself. I started to cast my mind back to when I met David. I was only twenty when I got married. It seemed this was the first time that I'd had a chance to look back over it all.

"Before I knew where I was, I was in the church. The choir was rehearsing for evening mass and I knelt down and listened to the beautiful music, the beautiful, true sounds. And I suddenly I was crying."

She raised her voice and looked at me.

"Because I realised that my life and everything about it was a lie. A poor lie put together for the sake of convention. I can't go back. I can't look them in the face.

"Why not, Madeleine? People change. Marriages end."

She didn't seem to hear me. "If I go back they'll know everything by looking in my eyes. Everything will fall apart."

"So what if it does?"

"I don't think everything should fall apart because I know too much."

"Hasn't your husband looked for you?"

"Oh yes, of course. He's been here twice, begged me to come home. I keep telling him that I can't, that

I'm not ready. That I need to be left alone to think things through. But it was a life I never should have had. I'll never go back to it."

She pulled herself together suddenly, got up, walked purposefully away. Poor, honest, confused woman. It was one of the saddest stories I had ever heard. We wandered desultorily round the Vatican apartments, we visited the Sistine chapel. I compared Madeleine silently to Michelangelo's lady, and saw there was more life in the painting. It was before the ceiling was restored, but still I saw the energy, the humanity, the truth of Michelangelo's figures, painted before the Renaissance stiffened into pretty pictures and whipped cream clouds. Fuck them, I thought, fuck my parents. I will do Art. We need it to fight the empire of lies. As I stepped with Madeleine into the pink Roman evening I said, "The Vatican bank is a major investor in the company that produces the contraceptive pill."

Madeleine smiled, but she said nothing. There were nets spiralling out from the cupola of St Peter's and from turrets and spires of every type, spreading a web of silence over the known world.

Strays

F our women sat about a white-clothed table, two old and two young, two mothers and two daughters. Mrs Doyle held Mrs Mooney's hand now and Dolores Mooney studied her nails, but Angela Doyle just lit a cigarette and let the voices lap in on her.

"He wanted for nothing at home anyway," said Mrs Doyle.

"I can't help blaming myself, Marion," said Mrs Mooney. "I can't help asking myself, did I show him enough love?"

"As much as it was humanly possible to show, Maeve. Don't go on destroying yourself like this. There's some things have no explanations, we have to endure them as best we can."

"I used get irritated with him sometimes, though, when he'd be sitting there, night after night…"

"I know, Maeve."

"He never seemed to have any desire to go out and enjoy himself or get himself a girlfriend like Declan did. He was always watching TV, or just sitting there alone in his room. God knows what he was doing in there year after year, Marion…"

Angela stretched her burdened cigarette to the ashtray in the middle of the table, inadvertently spattering ash on the white cloth. Dolores looked at her accusingly for a second, and then Mrs Mooney began again. "I never thought it could lead to anything as…as horrible…"

"Easy Maeve, easy. Don't keep thinking about it like that. Please God he's in a better place now anyway."

"He'd say he was 'low' he'd call it—but I never took him seriously. I had no idea, Marion."

"Of course you didn't. Come on, Maeve, there's no use breaking down again. Pour your mother another cup of tea, Dolores."

"Will you have some more tea, Mam?" said Dolores. Mrs Mooney nodded and wiped her face and Dolores poured.

Angela felt no grief. In fact, what she felt was mild irritation. Here they were, forced to mouth on about Gabriel all day, when they wouldn't have thrown him a spare thought if he'd been alive. She had never known him really. The two families were in and out of each other's houses every day of Angela's twenty-eight years, but it was Declan who had made the visits interesting. Declan was on his way back from Australia, in mid-air over India this very minute, maybe. She wondered idly had he changed: was he tanned or bearded, or was his hair sun-bleached? She and Declan had been very fond of each other. He had got married the year before—it was one of those things. Maureen was very nice. She wasn't saying anything, it was just she'd always hoped maybe something would come of her friendship with Declan. But Gabriel was a different story. He was short and twisted, as if he'd been crumpled in the making. And he had a twisted personality, secretive and joyless. Most of the time he was silent, and when he did speak, it was to complain about something. He was very good at his job, something to do with surveying. But then he would be, he was so exact all the time. Well, he'd been exact about the sleeping pills too. He'd gone about the thing with his usual thoroughness. Now he was waste matter and it fell to them to bury him as best they could. They would sit around the table and certain words would be said and then they would get up and he would be washed away.

Mrs Mooney quietened. She sipped at her tea. "If only I knew there was something special troubling him last night."

"Claire Higgins rang this afternoon, Mam, I didn't tell you."

"Who's Claire Higgins, love?"

"A girl who works in the bank with me. She's terribly upset about Gabriel."

"She knew him?"

"Not really. She knew him to see, that's all. He was interested in her, I suppose."

Angela saw her mother's face stiffen. You didn't talk about dead people and the opposite sex in Mrs Doyle's view of things. Dead people were pure and sexless, like angels on Christmas trees.

"Well, Gabriel used come into the bank," went on Dolores. "He didn't say anything, but whatever way he arranged it, he had some sort of business to do in there every day, and he always made sure he went to Claire. We used to wait for him to come in. It was a bit of a joke. We used swap round our tea breaks, and he'd look disgusted if he came in and she wasn't there. He'd get used to the new time, and we'd swap round again..." Dolores suppressed a giggle and then looked round quickly for forgiveness. When she got none she grew defensive. "It was only a bit of fun. We have to have something to keep us going in there. He went on in such a queer way."

"It takes all sorts, Dolores," said Mrs Doyle reproachfully.

"I suppose so. Claire liked him all right, she thought he was a laugh the way he went on. It was all a misunderstanding."

"What was?" asked Mrs Doyle, alarmed. Angela grew interested.

"She said if she'd known he was trying to ask her out, she would have gone. But how was she to know? He just kept saying he was going to the pictures on Saturday—he never said anything about taking her. Finally she got embarrassed. Anyone would have. She said she thought she'd go bowling herself. We were all having a bit of a giggle watching them, but then Gabriel turned round and walked out. Claire says she didn't know what she'd done."

This was new, thought Angela. She'd never really associated Gabriel with romance. He was always so gruff with women, as if he had better things to do than talk to them, like his surveying or whatever it was. But there was a memory butting at her consciousness. What was it? The holiday? Ten years ago? It was trying to come up, it was struggling against being washed away. What was it exactly?

"Claire's a lovely girl," went on Dolores. "She never would have meant any harm."

"We know that, Dolores. It was Gabriel's sickness made it hard for him to put himself across. That's what finished him in the end. It was no-one's fault."

It suddenly seemed only fair to Gabriel to remember well. Why would they not shut up for one minute and let her think? What was it exactly? A dark room and a chink in the curtain. Gabriel hadn't gone swimming, he was sick with sun-stroke. Angela'd bolted into the bedroom instead of the bathroom and Gabriel'd been sitting up, watching the girls getting dressed after their swim. And what she had seen had shocked her, she'd backed out immediately and shut the door. She had never opened it since.

"What made him the way he was, do you think?" Mrs Mooney was asking.

"There's no use us puzzling over that. Maybe he wasn't made for this world. He's gone where no-one will trouble him any more."

"I suppose you're right, Marion."

"Well," said Mrs Doyle placatingly, "you've two children credits to their mother anyway. Look at Declan, married to a lovely girl and managing his own chain of garages out in Australia. And look at Dolores, earning a good living in a steady job, and pretty as they come."

Mrs Mooney smiled at Dolores. "She's got the beauty alright," she said, and patted her daughter's thick, red hair.

"God sends us both trouble and joy, Maeve," went on Mrs Doyle. "You're going through your trouble but you'll have your joy as well. Please God the next time Declan and Maureen come back from Australia it will be for a happier occasion."

She beamed meaningfully at Dolores, who smiled.

"Well," said Mrs Mooney, "we all think Owen's a lovely boy, and Dolores knows nothing would please me more."

"That will be a happy day for us all," said Mrs Doyle.

There was a moment. Mrs Mooney shifted in her chair. Then she smiled and said, "Angela'll not be long going too, I suppose." Angela bit her lip and looked down. Mrs Doyle laughed quickly and Dolores refolded her legs and threw back her beautiful hair.

Angela walked out into the half-light and made quickly towards the sea. Perhaps her barely muttered excuse about fresh air had sounded rude, but she didn't care. They made her sick with their hypocrisies, their favouritisms. Maybe Gabriel had been right to rid himself of it all for good. Maybe Gabriel had seen that he had no place in it all. She reached the beach, eerie now in the almost dark, and sat on the cold, concrete promenade, looking out. "I understand you now," she said aloud, and wondered who she said it too. Then she realised she was speaking to Gabriel. God, if only she had given it time. With imagination and gentleness maybe…

All at once Gabriel was so close she could touch him. She reached out and began to untangle his twisted body. It was so easy and it didn't hurt at all. Gabriel was smiling now and he looked so different. Why had she gone wild for Declan like every other woman in Dublin when Gabriel was waiting for her, could have been hers? My God, it's not as if she had no need of some one. He could have been with her all this time. They could have defied the lot of them. They could have found their own place outside those limits, and made each other happy.

Angela got up suddenly and jumped onto the sand and began to run, but she stumbled and was forced to slow down, look where she put her feet. She saw then that the beach was littered with every kind of refuse, tin cans, a nappy, gobbets of sewage. And she had to stop, the cigarettes slowed her and then the excess weight as well. Her thoughts slowed and came clear. She had only been running to keep them off. It was time she stopped having these pathetic dreams. It would not have been possible. Just because Gabriel was ugly didn't mean he would have wanted what no-one else had. No-one ever would. She was so stupidly fat, you see, fatter than you can imagine. She was so fat that no-one would ever want her. She noticed a dark shape on the beach and quickly climbed the steps to the promenade. The place was full of winos from the shelter up the way, and she recognised the local flasher. Before she went back towards the house she saw him turn away from her. And he opened his coat and gave himself to the dark and the sea and the gulls.

Rest

She was walking towards Howth over the silver-sheeted sands at Sandymount, holding some big tall man by the hand. They walked and walked but they never seemed to get any closer, and then the rain drove in on their faces, and the sea began to swell, and the sand went to mud, so that they could hardly shift their legs in it, until they were sinking in it, up to their knees, their mouths, until they could breathe no longer...

Eleanor jerked her eyes open. It was always the same lately if she tried to sleep. There was this horror of suffocation. The dream was always basically the same, it was a dream of sinking, but the props and settings varied. It was difficult to say where this particular one came from, whether it was drawn from the book Eleanor had just edited, or whether it was a childhood memory, or whether it was both.

She had to sleep. She had a crucial meeting to-morrow with the chairman and board of the publishing house, and she had to be up at six to organise her notes. She had only had her job as commissioning editor with the new Irish literature department for a few months, and it was important that she make an impression. Perhaps it was knowing that the pill was there that kept her awake. If there weren't the possibility of that sureness perhaps sleep would come naturally. She checked the clock, two o'clock in the morning already. She crushed her eyes closed again and vowed not to move. If she lay very still and kept her eyes closed for long enough, perhaps she would eventually fall asleep.

Eleanor did not seem the sort to be prey to irrational fear. She was a successful woman. But it is true that success had come to her slowly. She just hadn't wanted the responsibility of an important position, but the opening of a new Irish literature department had been announced on her thirty-seventh birthday, and she had felt it was an omen. She knew she would be offered the position, she was the obvious choice; her qualifications were much higher than those of almost anyone else in the house, and then of course, she was Irish. The offer duly came, and she accepted. Then the fear had started, the carousel in her mind of endless alternatives, the terrible feeling of guilt.

On the face of it, she had little reason for guilt or fear, and much reason for pride. Eleanor had always fought her own battles. She hated to ask for anything and she hated to feel grateful. She had got through college on scholarships and prizes and it gave her great satisfaction that she didn't owe her superior education to her parents. She tried not to think of her parents and so she was glad there was no debt. That part of her life was over and she had started afresh. There was no need ever to re-open the wounds.

The wounds were deep but simple. Her mother had started drinking for no apparent reason when

Eleanor was ten. Of course, she hadn't known at first, and then she hadn't understood; there was just this badness, this hush. She hated her mother for it. She refused to be implicated. Her father said nothing specific, he just tried, silently, to make it up to her. But the silence made that impossible. Because nothing was officially wrong, it was difficult to make it right, or even better. Her mother had begun to hate the taciturn, pale-faced child who was so routinely dutiful and so ridiculously brilliant. The strain began to tell on her father's health, and eventually he had to leave the running of his antiquarian bookshop to an incompetent assistant. Then there was the drain of her mother's drinking, and the family was reduced to something approaching poverty. Her father watched the accounts growing more and more unbalanced and could do nothing. Eleanor could do nothing either. She went to school and did her homework—that was her only role. When she was about fifteen, her father went into hospital. He only recovered enough to apologise briefly before dying.

Everything around Eleanor might break and fall to pieces, but she would not. She closed her eyes to the bedlam, the weeping, the bringing to earth, she stuck out the two years it took to finish school. Her father had bequeathed the shop to his bookish daughter and their solicitor arranged for it to be sold to pay the debts. It fetched a great deal more than expected, mainly because of the books themselves, which Eleanor's father's infallible eyes had selected, but which his customers' could not. Eleanor was very mature for her age. She soon became a familiar face at the bank, withdrawing weekly a set amount of interest. With this she bought the necessities of life for herself and her mother, but of course, no drink. Her husband's death had changed her mother, anyway. She would talk to him urgently all day, explaining herself, asking forgiveness. She would sit weeping over the wedding photographs until Eleanor had to put cotton-wool in her ears to get to sleep. Mrs Kelly became a daily mass-goer and one of the other parishioners befriended her and tried to help. She introduced her to her sister, a kind, intelligent nun with the medical missionaries, who understood drink and guilt, bereavement and suffering. Whatever she said, it worked. Eleanor's mother was now as hooked on religion as she had been on drink. Eleanor found the loud, passionate rosaries almost as infuriating as the drunken tantrums, but they were safer. This was a comfort to her when she left.

She escaped to England as soon as she could. She was a gifted student and she succeeded fantastically, but she never seemed to glean much satisfaction from her success. Her beauty began to assert itself too, almost against her will. But she didn't do that well with the opposite sex, perhaps because she was so difficult to talk to. She was happiest when she could talk at you, about something of which you were ignorant. Because she could not be intimate, she did not inspire the thought of physical intimacy, except in those who saw her fleetingly, and from far away.

She did try to fall in love once, with a man from work, when she was in her late twenties. He was one of the few who ever wanted her badly because he thought he saw something in her which only he could release. She tried to fall in love with him, but it was the fall she feared most. There was no security of finding herself down there. She felt only relief when she finally shut the door on him. He left work, and found a job somewhere up north.

Fear was growing now in Eleanor's mind, and she saw little point in keeping her eyes closed. She always kept a night light burning in her room and now she fixed her eyes on its flicker, and her thoughts automatically wound back through the day. It had been unusually difficult. She was sitting in the common-room before nine, when the chairman Bernard Davis muttered, "So much for the first offering from the New Irish Writers' series."

Eleanor tried to make herself strong. She looked up and took the outstretched journal. Yes, it was a very bad review. The author was an unknown, but Eleanor had really believed in the book. That desperate man striding out across Sandymount strand and stepping over into heaven. How could anyone fail to be moved? She calmed herself. There were plenty of other papers. Reviews were not everything, anyway, and even if they lost a bit on the book in the short-term, Eleanor was convinced that having been the first to publish it would one day be important to the house.

She met Bernard's eyes and smiled. "Naturally, I don't agree with the reviewer. I think it's as good a new novel as I've read all year"

"We're not running a children's publishing venture, Miss Kelly." Bernard rattled his newly opened *Times*.

"Have adults no further need of the fantastic? Surely we need dreams more and more as we get older and wiser."

"I hope you're right. The readers consult the reviewers, not the publishers, you know."

Bernard was a pathetic, stupid little man. There was no need to get upset. Then Peter turned from the window. His eyes were like metal, shining but impermeable. Eleanor always felt he was laughing at her. Never more than now. "Maybe Miss Kelly wrote it herself and published under a pseudonym. That's why she's defending it like a mother."

"I'm always committed to fresh new writing, especially if, like this novel, it goes back and rediscovers the meaning of fiction, the satisfying of an emotional need."

"What about intellectual needs?" put in Bernard.

"Are the two to be separated? Not if what you call intellectual truly is that, and not dry posturing and pettiness."

"Definitely your own," interrupted Peter, laughing.

Eleanor was flushed. Her eyes stung and she dug her nails into the armrests. It would pass, she told herself. And it did pass. Nobody had noticed. But soon enough, somebody would notice. She didn't know why she let herself care so much what they thought. Bernard was an embarrassment to everyone. He was practically a figurehead; the staff his father had appointed ran the place. Peter was ten years younger than she, and got his kicks from chasing women ten years younger again. He always came very close to her when she handed her his work. Laughing at her. Why wouldn't he laugh at her? She had nothing to silence them with. She was successful but Peter knew how little that was worth—how little she was worth. He noticed her pathetic defensiveness, how she took every criticism as a personal insult. He noticed her nervousness when she asked him to do anything. He always did it, but his eyes said, if I contradict you, you will be powerless. It was true. She was just not suitable for the job. This was the third night of sleeplessness in a row.

She sprang out of bed and padded into the kitchen to get a glass of water and then back through the living-room towards the bathroom where she kept the pills. She had left the night light behind in the bedroom, the sitting-room was totally dark, and she stood still for a moment and listened anxiously for an unfamiliar sound. She had not been frightened of the dark as a child, it was something that had grown in her as an adult, living alone. She could hear nothing, and she prepared to go on, but glancing around the room she noticed a thickening in the darkness, an irregularity. She looked more carefully, there was a shape on the couch, a casually thrown coat or dressing-gown. She stooped to pick it up, but the darkness rose with a will of its own, holding its arms out to her. The glass dropped from her hands and cracked on the carpet, the water seeped out. Eleanor began to run, and she ran to the bathroom because there was a lock on the door. But when she pushed the door she met resistance, the hands of the darkness pushing against hers. She pushed desperately but she couldn't move the door, and finally she knew there was no hope. The darkness touched her and pulled her towards it. She was not crying. She had always known she would come face to face with terror.

"Please don't hurt me."

"Would I hurt you?"

She knew the voice. This was the terror then.

"Who are you?"

"Don't you know?"

He pulled back into a shaft of lamplight. He was unchanged, but his smile was freer. His hand was warm on her shoulder.

"You recognise me now."

"No I don't. I can't recognise you."

"I can see recognition in your face."

"There is none."

The man's face crumpled with pain, his fingers tightened on her. "Please Ellie. Don't say you've forgotten me so soon."

"You can't be him!"

"You remember me!"

"I remember my father."

"You remember me!"

Something strange happened to Eleanor. She trembled slowly and then terror shot through her and she screamed, "Christ no! Don't take me back with you, wherever you come from!"

"I'm your father! I couldn't hurt you, Ellie."

She tried to struggle away but he held her firmly and finally she screamed, "Why couldn't you have stayed where you were?" The fingers loosened. Eleanor had never heard her father cry. There was this terrible sound, like a wounded dog. She was ready to run away, but she couldn't do it, not when he seemed so human and so hurt. She said softly, "Dad," and touched him.

He said, softly too, "You recognise me now."

She nodded and moved towards him and there

was a tug in her she had not felt for many, many years. It was almost painful because she was so unaccustomed to it. His arms fastened around her and the luxury of it overcame her, the tears welled up in her eyes. He had his face against her and he said, "I knew you wouldn't reject me."

The questions went silent in her mind with the nearness of him. She realised she had always known he was there, somewhere. He brushed his hands through her hair and touched her shoulders. "You've grown up."

"I'm growing old."

"What age are you now?"

"Thirty-seven."

"You're beautiful even if you are like me. The women in my family were always beautiful. But somehow I never pictured you like this."

She took his hand and led him to the couch. They sat down and he put his arm gently around her. She said, "I can't remember us ever sitting like this."

"Poor Ellie. We were always rushing, whatever our problem was." He looked around, noted the bookcases lining the walls. "You love books too. That was obvious even when you were a child."

"Many of them are yours. I took my favourites away with me." She hesitated, then admitted, "I sold the shop."

"It had to go, Ellie, don't feel bad."

"I work for a publisher now."

"A publishah! You've nearly lost your Irish accent. I suppose you had to."

Eleanor laughed. "I suppose I did."

"But are you happy?"

"Not as happy as when I was a child...running along the strand with you and the dog, remember? I've never been truly happy since then."

"Well, it's a different sort of happiness."

"Unhappiness."

They laughed, but then he asked urgently, "Do you mean that?"

"It's not as strong as unhappiness. It's just a sense of being worthless, of ticking over for the sake of it. Boredom...and loneliness."

"You feel like that tonight, perhaps."

"No, it's not a feeling, it's knowledge. I've worked and worked, but I've somehow missed the point. It was just a simple mistake, but now it's too late to do anything."

"It's too late for me, Ellie. You have time. You're my greatest hope, you know."

"God help you."

"Stop talking like that. You have everything... looks...and brains. Every teacher you ever had said so."

"They always say that. It's to keep you paying the fees."

"Don't be sarcastic. I had every reason to be proud."

"I'm not denying that."

"Then what are you saying?"

"I started out well, I'll grant you that. But things have gone wrong since I've been left to my own devices. It's sad but it's a fact."

"You're not trying."

"Oh God, don't say that to me."

"Does it ever cross your mind that you're the only

continuation of my life and flesh? You have a responsibility to me in how you use your life. I fought to make your life possible. I remember clutching you at the cliffs of Moher, you kept wriggling, wanting to go nearer the edge."

"I'm sorry I've disappointed you."

"It's easy to say 'I'm sorry.' It's not good enough. Can you imagine how 'sorry' I am that my only descendant says her life's not worth having? You're alive! That's all you need. Get down and make an effort now."

"Don't dare ask me to try harder. God knows I've tried and it's all ended in humiliation. I've not told you in detail all the times I've tried to do something wild and different, or to bring some one into my life, and how I've suffered for it, and how disappointed I am. People don't care if you're trying, they judge you just the same. I should stand up to them, but I'm frightened of them. I'm too frightened and I'd rather admit that and settle to a modicum of comfort than give them a chance to laugh at me."

She felt him weaken beside her, sink in on himself, but his hand kept running through her hair, tremulously now. Then he said, "I thought I'd see you graduate from college, settle down. When that didn't happen, I consoled myself by thinking you were already strong enough when I left you. But you weren't, and they beat you down, the bastards."

"None of it's your fault."

"I didn't finish my work as a father, you don't seem to have any understanding of my love for you. There's no way of repairing the damage now."

He seemed so defeated. He had no future except

hers, and she saw him look out on nothingness. That was death: no future. He seemed to relax into death. She would have said anything to bring him back. She took his hand. "I suppose it's not hopeless, Dad. It's just the last few days I've been having a bit of trouble at work. I suppose I got depressed. I've been successful. You noticed the flat?"

"It's not hopeless." He repeated it like a mantra. "It's not at all hopeless. What kind of trouble at work, Eleanor?"

"I lack judgement. I've just published a novel, I thought it was the best thing I'd read in years. They say it's 'morbid' and 'psychotic.'"

"But they're wrong, aren't they?"

"I don't know. The thing just appealed to me, and I went ahead."

"That's judgement. I know you too well to doubt that it was good judgement."

"I'm not sure about it."

"Tell me the story."

"I'll tell you the ending. It's about this middle-aged man who had an industrial accident and lives on a disability allowance with his wife on the seafront at Sandymount. He feels worthless, his wife nags him incessantly. He has to drug himself to dull the pains in his arms and his legs. He can't go out, but every day he sits at his window and watches the light change on Howth across the strand. He says to his wife one morning, 'Could you walk to Howth across the sand, Biddy?'

'Sure what are you talking about,' says she. 'The sea comes in and cuts it off.'

'It looks like the sea has gone out to the horizon, it's

flat sand all the way. If you hurried when it was like that...'

She turns annoyed, to her washing. But he keeps looking at Howth gleaming like heaven, and one day when the pain has been bad and he's had to kill it as best he can, he lets himself out the front door when she's out shopping. He crosses the road, and he keeps walking. The tide is right out, he walks easily on the hard-packed sand. He walks a very long time, Howth doesn't get any nearer. He doesn't notice anything until suddenly the water begins to splash in over his shoes. He looks back a moment, but the house is hopelessly far away, and he knows he must push on and try to reach Howth. The water reaches his knees, his waist, and the sun keeps going down and the water reaches his neck and his mouth and the world goes dark. The sun has disappeared. The man walks up the beach at Howth and the sun is bright and hot, and the birds are clamouring."

She stopped and looked at him expectantly.

"Is that the end?"

"Yes."

"It's lovely."

"Is that how it is when you die?"

"That's how it is when you talk to me, it's the step on to Howth. You have to try to imagine death, whereas we have no more imagining to do."

She didn't really understand, but she smiled. They sat there in silence and this great lassitude came over her, she couldn't beat it back. Her head fell onto his chest and her ear pressed against his heart, which soothed her with its loud, hypnotic beating. Her eyelids closed, but a few seconds later she forced them open again, and found he was putting her down on the couch gently, so as not to wake her.

"Don't do that."

"You need to sleep."

"No, I want to talk."

"You're exhausted."

"You want to leave me."

"I don't want to leave you. I promise I'll stay."

She held both his hands and let her eyes close again. It was luxurious, slipping into that deep sleep. She tightened her fingers at intervals to check, but his hands were still there. She slept more deeply than she had done since she was a child and didn't wake until the first light of the November morning hit her eyes. She came to herself by degrees and holding tight to her father's hands, she pulled herself upright. He was still there and he smiled at her. He bent forward and kissed her cheek. Then his hands seemed to slip from her grasp. She trembled; she was losing him; he was fading as the light strengthened. She lunged forward to trap him in her arms and said, "You promised not to leave me."

But he said, "I only came because you had no belief in me; I'm with you when you believe it." And then her arms cut the air and the only body she held was her own.

She knew there was no use searching or pleading or shouting. There was nothing anyone could do to make up the loss. There was nothing she could do either. She felt anger at having to suffer that pain. Why had he come back if only to leave her again? The tenderness she felt now made the loss so much greater. Perhaps he had wanted that, the dead do not like to be forgotten. Or perhaps she had had a beautiful dream, of the kind only children have, or allow themselves to remember.

She went into the bedroom and lay down and slowly she began to cry, until she was howling like a child, with clenched fists. She cried and cried until she grew tired and could cry no more. Gradually her mind began to settle back on the morning. There was this terribly important meeting she needed to be up for, there was so much she had to do. She looked around for the clock and finally found it face down on the carpet, its alarm knocked off. It shuttled across the table when it rang, but she always cut it off before it reached the edge. This time its warning had gone unheard. It was half-past eight and there was so much she had to do.

Automatically, she sprang out of bed and put on the clothes she had laid out so carefully the night before. Then she ran into the bathroom and washed the tear-stains from her face with splashes of cold water. She began to drag a brush through her hair and she looked up at the mirror. She stopped and straightened herself. Her face was pink with deep sleep, with crying and with cold water and her hair hung around her shoulders. She smiled and the mirror face smiled back. Her father had been right. Though she was no longer a pretty girl, there was this consolation; she was a lovely woman. She took a clasp from the window-sill and began to pull her hair back into it, but suddenly she let it all go again. She didn't care if loose hair looked wrong with a suit. She didn't care. If she rushed now she could still make it in by nine. But she felt hungry. She went into the kitchen and brewed herself a pot of strong coffee and toasted herself two chunks of wholemeal bread. She smothered them in butter and honey and sat down to eat, trying to understand. She could understand none of it. She had never been more confused in her life. But she was not frightened. It was nearly an hour later when she roused herself and wandered towards the tube.

Peter looked up, surprised by her lateness and her appearance, but then greeted her in his usual resounding way, "Good morning, Miss Kelly." She just smiled and fumbled for her office key. She closed the door and began trying to organise her notes, but she could still feel the warmth of his hands in hers, she could concentrate on nothing else. She moved to the window and slumped into one of the wire basket chairs she had set informally at a coffee-table to put clients at their ease. She gazed down the road at the cars, the people, silenced by the double glazing, and soon she found she was crying again, weakly and quietly. She let the tears roll down her face, making no effort to stop them, unconscious of the time passing. The door opened suddenly and she raised her hands to wipe her face dry, but it was too late.

"Still not at your desk, Miss Kelly? Well, some of us have to work. Anything you want me to look over for the meeting?"

She looked up. Peter's smile snapped off like a light. Then he said, "Oh, I'm sorry." Immediately he became embarrassed. He had denied himself the possibility of not noticing. "Will I come back later?"

"Maybe if you could."

He moved a few paces. Then he turned back,

struggling, "Is anything wrong?"

"It's nothing. Thanks, Peter."

He hesitated. "Look, I'm no good at...If there's anything I can do...?"

He looked miserable. Eleanor took pity. "I suppose you could get us both a cup of machine-made coffee."

He smiled. "Biscuits?"

"Yes, why not some soggy biscuits as well. Make a party of it."

He hurried out into the corridor and came back with a plastic tray. He set it down and sat opposite her in the other wire basket chair, busying himself with the sugar and cream packets. He handed her her coffee. There was silence for a moment; they could find nothing to say to each other. Peter made an effort. "Are you planning to hit us with any more magical tales this morning?"

She smiled. "You don't find them as easy as that. Perhaps I've learned my lesson anyway."

"I hope not."

"The Doyle novel got slated."

"You didn't mind."

"I did."

"You shouldn't have. If I'd thought you minded I would have said something yesterday morning."

"Like what?"

"Like how much I enjoyed it myself."

"I wish you'd said that."

"I'm always watchful of what I say in front of Bernard. Like a fool."

Eleanor laughed and nodded. "I know...I can never scorn him as much as he deserves."

They smiled at each other and fell silent again.

Then Peter said, "What's on the agenda for the meeting?"

"I don't know."

He looked up sharply. "What do you mean?"

"I slept it in. It's not organised or typed up."

"But you have the ideas."

"Oh yes, of course. I spent nights working on this. But I can't present it because I didn't get up this morning." She gave a weak laugh.

"What are you going to do? Can you face them with nothing in type?"

"Not really."

"Couldn't we rush and get it done?'

"It's nearly eleven now. It's just too late."

He looked at her incredulously, her smile, her wild hair, her tear-stains. "I could ring now and say you're sick."

She seemed to enter into the spirit of this and nodded, "Yes, ring and say I've got 'flu."

Peter lifted the phone and dialed. Then she said firmly, "No. Say I can't make it for personal reasons."

It was too late to argue, Bernard's secretary was on the line, and Peter repeated what she wanted him to say. Eleanor heard the secretary's voice lift in surprise and then return to its tone of faceless tact. Then Peter put down the phone, and they began to giggle. They went quiet suddenly and Eleanor looked out the window again, a smile twitching on her lips and tears in her eyes. Peter had never seen her either happy or sad before, and now she was both. He bent forward and asked, "What's happened, Eleanor?"

She looked up at him and tried to speak; her raised eyes begged him to understand. She opened her mouth and drew breath slowly and said, "My father died when I was fifteen."

Peter didn't know what to say. It was a sentence of simple past description. But her face made him feel he must react differently, as if she had suffered the loss that very day. He said, "I'm sorry," and then felt silly, but he saw by her face that it was the right thing. Smiling, she leaned back unselfconsciously like a girl at school, and it seemed that she was held by invisible hands, but her toe just tipped his chair and balanced her.

Destiny of Dreams

by
Michael Bowler

A boy grows up in Cahirciveen with dreams of freedom but has to face the realities of life in Ireland in the 1950s.

A brilliant first novel: evocative, lyrical and passionate

POOLBEG

A Strange Kind of Loving

by Sheila Mooney

A touching, searingly honest and at times heartbreaking account of an upbringing in an Ascendancy family and the author's vain attempts to win the love and approval of her Victorian father while continuing to support her beautiful, eccentric and alcoholic mother. Sheila Mooney is the sister of 1930s Hollywood idol, Maureen O'Sullivan, and her memoir contains witty and illuminating accounts of her career.

POOLBEG

In Quiet Places

The Uncollected Stories, Letters and Critical Prose of Michael McLaverty

Edited with an Introduction by Sophia Hillam King

This collection provides a unique and fascinating insight into the mind and artistic development of one of Ireland's finest writers

POOLBEG

The Poolbeg Golden Treasury of Well-Loved Poems

compiled by
Sean McMahon

A delightful anthology of classic poetry

POOLBEG

Women Surviving
Studies in the History of Irish Women
in the 19th and 20th centuries

Edited by

Maria Luddy and Cliona Murphy

This highly original collection of historical articles addresses aspects of women's history in nineteenth and early twentieth-century Ireland, including: nuns in society; paupers and prostitutes; the impact of international feminists on the Irish suffrage movement and women's contribution to post-Independence Irish politics.

POOLBEG